THE DARKER SIDE OF LOVING

Amy had been through one traumatic relationship—she didn't want to ever face the pain of loss again. But Luke Tanner wouldn't take no for an answer, and she found that she didn't really want him to . . .

THE DARKER
SIDE OF LOVING

BY

YVONNE WHITTAL

MILLS & BOON LIMITED
15–16 BROOK'S MEWS
LONDON W1A 1DR

*First published in Great Britain 1986
by Mills & Boon Limited*

© Yvonne Whittal 1986

*Australian copyright 1986
Philippine copyright 1986
This edition 1986*

ISBN 0 263 75437 5

*Set in Monophoto Times 11 on 11 pt.
01-0886 – 53549*

*Printed and bound in Great Britain by
Collins, Glasgow*

CHAPTER ONE

THE late afternoon sun filtered through the venetian blinds at the windows of Aloe Tours (Pty) Ltd, and cast a zebra pattern of light and shadow across the carpeted floor. The muted sounds of traffic in Cape Town's busy Adderley Street drifted up to the offices on the fourth floor of the stone building, but Amy Warren did not hear it as she rose behind her desk with a file in her hands and walked into the adjoining office where her uncle was attaching his signature to the letters his secretary had typed. He looked up, taking in her small slenderness in the apricot-coloured suit and the black, wispy hair framing her attractive, delicately-boned features. There was an ethereal quality about her that attracted men at the first glance, but there was also a cool aloofness in the honey-brown eyes that held them at bay.

Benjamin Smythe smiled, his grey eyes crinkling deeply at the corners. 'If that's the list of bookings for tomorrow's tour of the winelands, then put it in the "in" tray and sit down.'

Amy did as she was told, and slipped her stockinged feet out of her black, high-heeled shoes to wriggle her toes under the desk. It had been one of those days when she had been on her feet more often than seated behind her desk, and she was tired. It was, however, a tiredness accompanied by a deep satisfaction. Four years ago her uncle had offered her this partnership in Aloe Tours, he had taught her everything she knew, and her life had taken on a new dimension which she would not exchange now for anything in the world.

'The economic recession is having a crippling effect on the industries, and it's murdering the smaller companies.' Ben Smythe put down his pen and leaned back in his chair with a sigh which indicated that he, too, was tired. 'The only thing that's still keeping our business alive is the fact that the rand has dropped in value, and as a result we're experiencing an influx of tourists into the country such as we don't normally have in South Africa.'

'This country has a tremendous amount to offer the tourist, but in some instances we lack the necessary facilities.' Amy's expression was grave. This was a problem she had wrestled with often during recent months. 'What we need desperately are well-organised, all-inclusive tours to the various places of interest.'

'To launch something like that could cost a small fortune,' her uncle argued, lacing his fingers together across his chest. 'To start off with we would need at least two luxury coaches to give the tourists the air-conditioned comfort they would require on a long trip in our hot, often humid climate, but the biggest problem would be to secure decent accommodation at a reasonable tariff. Families are opting for camping holidays since it's cheaper, and the hotels are practically empty. Everyone is fighting for survival, and the hoteliers have been forced to raise their tariffs to make ends meet which makes me doubt if they will look kindly upon a request for special rates.'

'I think you're being unduly pessimistic, Uncle Ben.' The corners of her soft mouth lifted in a smile which exposed the pearly-white sheen of her perfect teeth. 'We would be filling their hotels for them, and what they may lose on tariffs they will be amply compensated for in the extras which tourists usually require.'

'You have a point there, Amy, and I think it's worth following up.' Ben Smythe smiled, his greying head contrasting heavily with the black leather of his high-backed chair. 'You're a clever, bright young woman, and I think I'm getting too old for this business.'

'Nonsense, Uncle Ben!' Amy's soft laughter was pleasing on the ear, and there was a teasing light in her large, sometimes soulful eyes. 'For a man of fifty-five you play a mean game of tennis, and your mind is still as sharp as a razor.'

'I doubt if Dorothy will agree with you on the latter,' he grunted, reaching for his cigarettes and lighting one. 'For the first time in twenty-six years I forgot our wedding anniversary last month, and it took me a week to discover why I was being subjected to her icy glances.'

'Serves you right!' she admonished him playfully.

They smiled at each other across the width of his desk, then his expression sobered. 'You've been alone too long, Amy. It's time you found yourself a husband and settled down.'

Amy's long, dark lashes swept down to veil her eyes. This had become a ritual in recent months, and her body grew taut with resentment. 'This isn't the first time you've said that, and I wish you would believe me when I say that I'm perfectly happy the way I am.'

'It's been four years since——'

'I know!' There was a sharpness in her usually soft voice as she raised shuttered eyes to his. 'I know exactly how long it has been, but I've made a new life for myself, and I have no desire to change it.'

'You're twenty-six, Amy, and you're not getting any younger,' her uncle reminded her stubbornly.

'Good heavens, girl, soon there won't be any eligible men left for you to choose from, and you're much too pretty to be left on the shelf.'

'I have settled myself very comfortably on that shelf, darling Uncle Ben,' she smiled forcibly, hiding the memory of pain and suffering. 'And I happen to like it there,' she added for good measure.

'It's unhealthy to shut oneself away from a normal relationship with someone of the opposite sex,' he grunted, drawing hard on his cigarette and blowing a stream of smoke towards the white ceiling. 'Dammit, Amy, I know what a tough time you had, but you can't let it affect you for the rest of your life.'

'I'm happy the way I am, Uncle Ben, truly I am.'

'Who are you trying to bluff, my girl?' His disbelieving glance succeeded in holding hers. 'Me . . . or yourself?'

Amy felt as if she had been driven into a corner. If she was honest with herself then she would admit that she was not entirely happy. She was very often lonely, but loneliness was preferable to the anxieties she had suffered and the pain of eventual loss. She glanced at her watch, and pushed her feet into her shoes before she rose to her feet. 'I think it's time we closed up shop and went home.'

'I don't like what you're doing to yourself, Amy,' her uncle stopped her before she could leave his office. 'You have to accept the fact that fate sometimes deals us rotten cards. Life is mostly a gamble, you win some and you lose some, but you can't shut yourself away from it because of what happened to you in the past.'

'Thanks for the lecture.'

'All right, I get the message, and I know I always make you angry when I bring up this subject, but I happen to be concerned about you.'

During the ensuing silence only the muted hum of the traffic could be heard while Amy and her uncle faced each other across the length of his office. Her resentment drained away from her as always when she looked into his kindly eyes, and she crossed the room to his side in a few quick, graceful strides.

'I know you're concerned about me,' she said, her small hand gripping his arm as she bent down to kiss his cheek. 'The truth is I'm a coward, Uncle Ben, and I refuse to suffer the agonies of yet another rotten deal at the hands of fate!'

Amy awoke on the Friday morning with the distinct feeling that spring was in the air. She leapt out of bed in her Bellville flat, drew aside the curtains, and opened the window to let in the cool, fresh breeze. She drew the air deeply into her lungs while her glance rested on the majestic Table Mountain in the distance with its cloth of mist draped over it. This was the view that had greeted her every morning for the past four years and, whatever the weather, it had never failed to please her.

The long drive into the city that morning did not fill her with the irritation she sometimes encountered, and when she walked into her office her secretary, Penny Gibson, smiled at her from behind her typewriter.

'You look like an advertisement for spring,' she said, her glance sliding over Amy's slim figure in a coral pink linen dress with a wide, embroidered collar.

'There's a definite indication that spring is on

our doorstep,' Amy admitted. 'I can feel it tingling in my blood.'

'Are you sure you're not in love?' Penny teased lightly, and Amy's soft laughter rippled through her secretary's small office.

'I'm in love with the miracle of nature, yes,' said Amy, opening the door to her office and entering it with a light step at the knowledge that she did not have to accompany a tour group out to the winelands that morning.

There was a pile of paperwork on her desk needing attention, but her mood was too good to let it daunt her. There was also a pile of correspondence from the previous day and she quickly sorted the letters into some order before she buzzed Penny and asked her to come in.

The morning passed swiftly and smoothly. There were a few intricate matters she had to consult her uncle about before she made a decision, and he, too, seemed to have a strange air of excitement hovering about him.

'Do you have anything planned for this evening?' he asked after lunch that day when he entered her office through the interleading door.

'I've stacks of ironing to do.'

'You can do that over the weekend,' he brushed aside her statement. 'I've invited a couple of friends over to dinner this evening, and Dorothy and I would like you to be there as well.'

For some inexplicable reason she was instantly on the alert. 'I know this is an invitation, but you're making it sound very much like an order.'

'Shall we expect you at seven?' he asked, his smiling countenance giving nothing away.

'Yes, Uncle Ben,' she accepted, but not without a certain wariness. 'Thank you, I'll be there at seven.'

The door closed behind her uncle, and she stared at it for some time with a slight frown between her perfectly arched brows before she shrugged off her uneasiness and concentrated on her work.

Amy dressed with her usual care that evening. Her silk dress with the wide, lacy sleeves was the colour of jade, and on a slender chain about her throat hung a small diamond pendant in the shape of a heart. It glittered in the light against her creamy skin, and it was as cold as the heart that beat in her breast. She fingered the pendant lightly as she studied herself in the mirror, and pain mingled with the look of nostalgia in her eyes. It was the first expensive gift Keith had given her, and she could remember the occasion with agonising clarity. They had gone for a walk into the mountains he had loved so much. The cold wind had whipped his dark hair across his forehead, but there had been warmth and laughter in his blue eyes when he had taken the pendant out of his jacket pocket to fasten it about her throat.

'For ever,' Keith had said. 'You will be mine for ever.'

Two years later she was alone and lost, and the will to live had almost deserted her when her uncle uprooted her summarily and brought her to Cape Town.

Amy tried to force her thoughts back to the present, but her mind continued its relentless passage back into the past. She had been an only child, and she had adored her parents. Two days before her sixteenth birthday her father had died in a mine accident on the reef, and her mother had simply wasted away after his death, living long enough only to see her daughter through to her final year at school. It had been a tremendous blow to find herself on her own at the age of eighteen, but then there had been Keith Warren. Their families had lived right next door to each other, they had gone to school together, they had dated, and they had eventually drifted into a marriage which had been as comfortable as their friendship all through those adolescent years. Amy had been twenty, and Keith twenty-two. They had been young, but they had been happy, and they had worked hard at their life together.

Two years later he was killed when a freak storm washed away a bridge and took his car with it. Amy had been carrying his child at the time: it had been the only living thing she still had to cling to, but two weeks later she miscarried. Demented with shock, it had taken months of therapy before she was ready to face the world again, and the protective barriers she had built around herself then were still very much intact now. She would never love again. To love meant pain, and she had had her fair share of that.

She stared at her pain-filled eyes in the mirror, and succeeded at last in shutting out the past to concentrate on applying her make-up with a light hand. She was fortunate to have a healthy skin that needed no more than a moisturiser, a light dusting of power, and a touch of lipstick to give colour to her wide, sensitive mouth. Her shoulder-length black hair waved naturally, and swimming and tennis kept her body supple and trim.

She glanced at her watch. If she did not hurry she would be late and, snatching up her silk wrap and sequinned evening bag, she switched off the lights and locked the door to her flat securely behind her as she left.

Ben and Dorothy Smythe had a comfortable home in Table View with a swimming-pool and tennis court, and Amy was always a welcome guest at weekends when she had nothing better to do.

There were three cars parked in the cobbled courtyard of her uncle's home that evening, but one in particular caught her attention. It was a sleek red Ferrari, built for speed and comfort . . . and very expensive. Amy parked her metallic blue Toyota Avanti next to it, and she lingered for a moment in the lamp-lit darkness of the courtyard, her appreciative glance sliding over the gleaming bodywork of the Ferrari. Who on earth did it belong to?

The front door opened almost the instant her finger released the buzzer, and Ben Smythe ushered her into the comfortably and tastefully furnished living-room. Amy knew the Charltons and the Raubenheimers, they were old friends of her uncle's, and Aunt Dorothy's warm embrace was an equally familiar welcome.

'I'm so glad you could come, my dear,' her green eyes smiled into Amy's, then she glanced at her husband. 'Will you introduce her, Ben?'

Her uncle's hand on her shoulder made her turn, and at that moment a man rose from the depths of an armchair which had hidden him from Amy's view when she had entered the room. Her startled mind registered his identity at once when she encountered his deeply tanned, ruggedly handsome features. Luke Tanner was a businessman of repute, and his name was synonymous with that of the Blue Dolphin group of hotels. Amy had seen his photograph often enough in newspapers and magazines, and seldom without a beautiful woman at his side. His image on paper had suggested a ruthless vitality, but in the flesh he projected a raw, masculine appeal that left her feeling weak at the knees for the first time in her life.

'Amy, I'd like you to meet Luke Tanner,' Ben Smythe introduced her, his hand in the small of her back urging her forward. 'Luke, this is my niece, Amy Warren, and she also happens to be my partner in business.'

Tawny eyes smiled a long way down into hers with a deceptive laziness in their depths, and her small hand was engulfed in a firm, yet gentle grip that sent little sparks of electricity skipping across her nerve ends.

'It's a pleasure to meet you, Amy.'

His deep baritone voice sent another wave of weakness surging into her knees, and her own voice sounded stilted when she responded with a prim, 'How do you do?'

Amy carefully extricated her fingers from his hand. She was having difficulty in controlling that odd quickening of her pulses when her uncle interrupted the awkward little silence.

'There's something I must discuss with Harry Charlton before dinner,' he excused himself. 'Luke, be a good chap and get Amy a drink.'

'Certainly,' Luke Tanner agreed, the strongly chiselled mouth curving in a sensuous smile the moment they were alone. 'What will you have, Amy?'

Her name on his lips had a pleasant ring to it, and that quivering weakness inside her made her realise that the occasion demanded something stronger than soda and lime. 'I'd like a gin and tonic, thank you.'

Amy watched him walk away towards the mahogany bar with its mirrors and glass shelves. The expensive cut of his evening suit complimented his tall, wide-shouldered frame, and he exuded an aura of quiet authority which seemed to make him stand out from the rest of her uncle's guests. He was not as young as he appeared in many of his photographs, and she guessed his age at somewhere between thirty-five and forty. She caught a look in her uncle's eyes across the room, and knew at once that Luke Tanner was the reason she had been invited to dinner that evening. She resented it, and had difficulty in hiding her feelings when Luke Tanner returned to her side with a gin and tonic in one hand, and a glass of whisky in the other.

'How long have you been in partnership with Ben?' he questioned Amy when they were seated, his tawny eyes regarding her with undisguised interest.

'Four years,' she answered, gulping down a mouthful of gin and tonic to rid herself of those crazy butterflies in the pit of her stomach.

'Ben and I often play golf together, and I can't imagine why he never told me he had such a beautiful niece.' There was suddenly a certain intimacy in his appraisal. It was as if he was divesting her of her clothes with a slow, deliberate sensuality and, for the first time in years, she felt a wave of heat surging from her throat into her face. 'If Ben wasn't your uncle, and a married uncle at that,' he added mockingly, 'I'd be inclined to think he had jealously been keeping you all to himself.'

At any other time she might have been ready with a cutting reply, but her nerves had started to jump as if she had attached herself to an electrical circuit. She felt disarmed, completely unnerved, and she hastily swallowed down a second mouthful of gin and tonic, but as she did so she glimpsed that lazy, sensuous smile curving his mouth. This man was not inexperienced, he knew exactly what he was doing to her, and for some hateful reason he was enjoying her confusion and embarrassment.

'Please come through to the dining-room,' Aunt Dorothy announced, relieving Amy of the necessity to reply to Luke Tanner's remark. 'And please do bring your drinks through with you.'

To Amy's complete dismay, she found herself seated directly opposite Luke Tanner, and the evening took on the proportions of a nightmare. The Charltons and the Raubenheimers were charming people, but Amy found it difficult trying to concentrate on the conversation she was having with them while those tawny eyes opposite continued to observe her relentlessly. She felt her composure slipping and tried to ignore him, but Luke Tanner was a man who made his presence felt in no uncertain terms, and he constantly drew her into the conversation with nettling remarks that made her retaliate with an unaccustomed sarcasm and caused Ben and Dorothy Smythe to glance in her direction several times with a look of surprise on their faces.

The conversation inevitably took a swing towards the country's economic situation, and while the men became involved in a heated discussion, Amy took that brief opportunity to study the man seated opposite her.

His hair grew thick and strong from his broad forehead into his neck, and it was the colour of a lion's mane to match his eyes. His nose looked as if it could have been broken at some time, and his square jaw suggested that he was resolute and determined in everything he did. In retrospect he was not an extremely good-looking man, but Amy had to admit to herself that he had a magnetic personality which drew one's attention and held it.

'Our tours don't extend beyond Namaqualand, but there's a great need for expansion at the moment,' Amy heard her uncle saying.

'Do you still organise those day trips into the winelands?' Jack Raubenheimer asked in between mouthfuls of dessert.

'We do,' Ben nodded, dabbing at his mouth with his table napkin and leaning back in his chair. 'We are short of tour guides at the moment, and Amy has been taking the tourists on the twice-weekly trip into the Paarl district.'

Amy had become accustomed to having a certain amount of attention focused on her since she went into partnership with her uncle, but Luke Tanner's faintly mocking regard made her feel gauche.

'Are you an expert on wine, Amy?'

'No, Mr Tanner,' she answered coldly, resenting the feeling that he was belittling her capabilities. 'I leave that part of the tour to the guides at the wine estates we visit. They're the experts, and I would never dream of encroaching on their domain.'

There was laughter in his tawny eyes and in the curve of his sensuous mouth. If he was deliberately trying to annoy her, then he was succeeding admirably.

They returned to the living-room for coffee and liqueurs, and Amy was relieved when the men grouped themselves around Uncle Ben's bar, leaving the women to discuss their own particular interests.

Amy felt herself relax for the first time that evening, but when she rose to place her empty cup on the tray she found herself looking directly into Luke Tanner's eyes. His gaze was compelling, rendering her immobile as he detached himself from the men and walked towards her.

'Shall we take a stroll in the garden?' he invited, his hand sliding beneath the wide, lacy sleeve of her dress to grip her arm above the elbow so that a thousand little nerves leapt to attention.

'No, I don't——'

'Afraid of the dark?' he interrupted her refusal with a sardonic lift of his heavy eyebrows while his eyes challenged her.

'Of course not,' she accepted his challenge with some annoyance, and he escorted her out on to the darkened terrace.

It was an unusually warm night despite the playful breeze that tugged at the wide skirt of her dress and lifted her hair until it lay in slight disarray about her face. There was a crescent moon in the sky, and it lit their way as they walked down the stone steps and along the path towards the fountain spraying water into a fish pond directly below it. It was peaceful in the garden, but Amy felt incredibly tense and wary. Being alone with Luke Tanner intensified her awareness of that powerful magnetism he exuded, and the uncertainty of whether she could cope with it placed her at a disadvantage. She had never before had this unerring instinct that she was being threatened in some way, and it frightened her.

His hand released her arm when they reached the fountain, and her nerves settled themselves back into a facsimile of their usual order while she covertly watched him take a slim gold cigarette case from his pocket. He offered her one, but when she shook her head he lit a cigarette for himself, and his rugged features appeared harsh in the flame of his lighter.

'There's something I'd like to know, Amy.' She felt herself tense as she waited for him to continue. 'Do you dislike all men, or is there something about me in particular that you don't like?'

Amy was momentarily too startled to answer. Was that how he had interpreted her reaction? Perhaps that was the impression she had given while trying to fight off this powerful attraction she could not deny even to herself.

'I don't dislike you, Mr Tanner,' she made an attempt at setting the record straight.

'Would you explain to me, then, why I've had this feeling all evening that you resent my presence?'

That was true! She did resent his presence to some extent, and his ability to gauge her feelings angered and frightened her simultaneously. 'Perhaps you feel that way because you're accustomed to women who are only too anxious to capture your attention.'

'Perhaps,' he agreed with a hint of ice in his voice, 'but I must confess that your technique deserved an award for the unquestionable success you've had this evening in attracting my attention.'

'*That isn't*——' She stopped abruptly in her attempt to deny his remark when she realised that her personal attack had gone beyond the limits of their brief acquaintance, and she could not blame him for the manner in which he had retaliated. 'I suppose I deserved that,' she conceded with a faintly embarrassed smile.

'I think you did,' he underlined the fact gravely, then he smiled down at her from his great height. 'Shall we start all over again?'

'Why should we do that?' she asked warily, trying to concentrate on the tinkling fountain and not on the man who was suddenly standing so close to her that her senses were beginning to react in the most alarming way to his particular brand of masculine cologne.

'I'd like to get to know you better, Amy

Warren.' His baritone voice was like a soft caress trailing across the tips of her receptive nerves, and her alarm spiralled when he raised a hand to brush away that wisp of hair which the playful breeze had blown across her pink lips. 'I'd like to know what goes on in that beautiful head of yours, and to do that I shall have to see you more often.'

Amy felt a coldness shifting through her like a premonition of danger, and she shivered visibly in the darkness. 'I think I'd like to go inside.'

'Yes,' he agreed, crushing his cigarette into the grass beneath the heel of his expensive shoe, and taking her arm. 'It has suddenly become rather chilly.'

Curious glances were directed at them when they entered the house, especially from Uncle Ben and Aunt Dorothy, but Amy pretended not to notice, and Luke Tanner was quite unperturbed when he rejoined the men at the bar.

Amy somehow managed to get through the remainder of the evening, but she was determined to make her uncle understand that she did not approve of the methods he had employed in his attempt to find her a husband.

Luke Tanner was the last to leave that evening, and his parting remark filled her with an even greater uneasiness than before.

'We'll meet again, Amy,' he said, and he had turned to thank his host and hostess before Amy could formulate a contradictory reply.

Minutes later his red Ferrari roared out of the cobbled courtyard, and Amy felt her uneasiness being temporarily replaced by a fierce anger when she turned to see her uncle observing her speculatively.

'What did you think of Luke?'

'Never mind what I think of Luke Tanner!' she

stormed at him as they returned to the living-room. 'It would be more to the point to discuss what I think of *you* at this moment. You engineered this meeting between Luke and myself, and the rest of your guests were here simply for decoration in case I suspected, but I realised what you had been up to from the moment I walked in this evening.'

'All right, so you're angry with me,' Ben accepted her furious onslaught good-naturedly, 'but I'm merely helping you to meet people.'

'I'm meeting people almost every day in my job,' she reminded him caustically.

'That may be so,' her uncle shrugged, 'but they're people who come and go, and you never see them again.'

'That's the way I like it!'

'Amy!' he sighed exasperatedly. 'You can't go through life with nothing and no one touching your heart again.'

Only one man had ever succeeded in touching her heart. No one else could touch her heart again, and she had vowed that no one else would. 'I have the sole right to decide what is best for myself where my heart is concerned.'

There was a startled little silence which was broken by Aunt Dorothy's laughter as she linked her arm through her husband's. 'Darling, I think you're being told to mind your own business, and quite rightly too.'

'I know,' Ben nodded, a glimmer of hurt in his amused grey eyes.

'Uncle Ben . . .' Amy began contritely, and her honey-brown eyes were suddenly imploring. 'I know you mean well, but I wish you wouldn't.'

'Okay, so I won't do anything again to pressurise you, but what are you going to do about Luke?'

Amy stared at her uncle, her uneasiness returning in full force. 'What do you mean?'

'I heard what he said to you before he left here, and he isn't a man to make promises without following them through.'

Amy recalled Luke Tanner's words with frightening clarity, and quite suddenly it had sounded more like a threat than a promise. *We'll meet again.* His arrogant self-assurance had rankled, and she was determined to do everything in her power to avoid a second meeting.

'Luke Tanner will soon get tired of taking "no" for an answer,' she said when she realised that Uncle Ben and Aunt Dorothy were expecting her to say something.

They looked at her with an odd expression on their faces, as if they doubted her ability to hold out against a man like Luke Tanner, and on her way home some minutes later she realised that they probably had reason to feel that way. He had certainly had a devastating effect on her, and his determination was quite evident in everything she had read about him in the past, but Amy also had no reason to suspect that he would lose any sleep over her when there were so many other women only too eager to step into the proverbial shoes she had declined to fill.

She would cope. *Of course* she would cope, she told herself. During the past four years she had not exactly lacked male attention. There had been quite a few who had attempted to strike up a relationship with her, and she had had no difficulty in making them realise that she was not interested. Why, then, should she encounter any difficulty with Luke Tanner? The answer came without a great deal of mental exertion. Luke was a force to be reckoned with. He was not a man accustomed to failures, and he was not a man who would take kindly to having his plans thwarted.

Amy's fingers tightened on the steering wheel of her Toyota Avanti. She could not ignore that powerful attraction she had felt. It was something totally alien to her, and it frightened her that this man had it in his power to strip her almost completely of her composure. For the first time in her life she had been made intensely aware of the fact that she was a woman, that her femininity could attract and arouse a man's interest. She had been made to feel vulnerable in Luke Tanner's presence, and also uncertain of herself. This instant physical attraction was something that confused and bewildered her. It was something she would have to guard against, or she might become her own worst enemy. She did not want to become involved with a man. She did not want a relationship which might lead to the need for a commitment, and she had no intention of laying herself wide open to the agonies she had suffered once before.

There was a darker side to loving, she had walked through that valley four years ago, and she had come close to losing her mind. She had vowed afterwards never to feel so strongly about anyone again. To care aroused a suffering of its own kind, and to lose the one you care for intensifies that suffering until it becomes a searing agony. Uncle Ben had said that she could not go through life with nothing and no one touching her heart, but that was the only way she could face life with a semblance of serenity.

'We'll meet again, Amy.' Luke Tanner's words echoed mockingly in her ears. No doubt they would meet again, but this time she would be prepared for it instead of caught unawares. She would fight that attraction, it was purely physical after all, and with her mind in control she would be assured of a victory.

CHAPTER TWO

AMY walked towards the Aloe Tours' coach parked outside the Airways Terminal in the Heerengracht. It was a sunny September morning, spring was in the air, and there was a slight buoyancy in her stride as she mounted the steps into the coach with her clipboard in her hand.

'How many passengers do we have, Bill?' she checked with the coach driver to make sure that all twenty-six passengers listed had boarded the coach.

'Twenty-seven this morning,' he answered, and Amy's dark brows lifted in surprise as she cast a swift glance down the length of the coach.

'Twenty-seven? We're only supposed to have——' Her voice faded abruptly and her heart missed a suffocating beat when her glance collided with Luke Tanner's amused, tawny gaze. He was seated in the rear of the coach, and somehow she found herself walking towards him down the aisle. The passengers turned in their seats as she walked past them, their curious glances following her, but Amy was oblivious to everything except that slow anger simmering inside her. She paused in front of him, her angry glance taking in the open-necked shirt exposing his strong throat, the blue, tailored jacket, and the immaculate grey slacks encasing his long, muscular legs. 'What are you doing here?' she demanded in a furious, but hushed voice.

His mouth curved in a sensuous smile, and his glance shifted slowly down her body as if he was probing beneath her neat, pale green suit and crisp white blouse. 'I said we would meet again, didn't I?'

'Your name was not on the list of bookings yesterday,' she pointed out icily, ignoring his remark.

'I asked them not to attach my name to that list.'

'It's against the regulations,' she accused, her hands clutching the clipboard against her breast as if it afforded her protection against those eyes which were so intent on stripping her of her clothes as well as her composure. 'But I imagine your requests are always granted.'

'Nearly always,' he agreed ironically, but with a hint of censure in his deep voice. 'Does my presence bother you?'

'Not at all,' she lied, while everything inside her cried out the opposite.

'Then isn't it time the coach departed?' he asked, consulting the expensive gold watch strapped to his strong wrist.

Amy felt as if she had been rapped over the knuckles for neglecting her duties, and she could barely conceal her fury as she spun round and walked down the aisle towards her seat up front with the driver. She indicated to Bill that they could go, and they were moving out of the Heerengracht before Amy had calmed herself sufficiently to lift the microphone off its hook and rise to her feet so that she was facing the passengers. She could not avoid being aware of Luke Tanner regarding her intently from the rear of the coach, and she found that the only way she could cope with her duties was to concentrate on the passengers closest to her.

She raised the microphone, bringing it close to

her lips, and a faint crackling sound echoed throughout the coach when she flicked the switch. 'Good morning, ladies and gentlemen,' her voice emerged from the speakers with a calmness she was far from experiencing. 'My name is Amy, your driver is Bill, and we welcome you to Aloe Tours.'

The passengers responded spontaneously to her greeting and, knowing that she had captured their attention, she continued to explain the nature of the tour.

'We are taking the main road to Paarl, and we shall be visiting two of the many wine estates in the Berg River Valley area. At each of these estates you will be taken on a guided tour of the wineries and cellars. You will also have the opportunity to sample and perhaps buy some of your favourite wines direct from the estates.'

Taking into consideration that most of the tourists were not South Africans, Amy related briefly some of the highlights of Cape Town's historical background, but when they were some distance out of the city her glance was drawn towards the tawny eyes observing her from the rear of the coach with a lazy, amused smile that affected her pulse rate, and she looked away again hastily.

The tour continued without a hitch, despite the fact that Amy's nerves had tangled themselves into a knot which was almost painful. There was an expectant murmur among the visitors as the first vineyards came into view, but spring had only just come and the vineyards were not yet at their best. The preceding winter had stripped the vines of foliage and the new growth was yet to appear with the sap rising in the stems, but this did not diminish the eagerness of the tourists.

There was a delay, however, as they approached Paarl on the N1. A fruit truck had overturned, and although the road was being cleared a congestion of traffic was building up on the north and southbound sides. Amy sensed an air of restlessness among the group, and stepped into the breach with a hasty improvisation.

'While we're waiting for the road to be cleared I could perhaps tell you a little of Paarl's history,' she said over the microphone. 'To your left you will see the Paarl Mountain with its three distinctive granite boulders which were named Paarl, Britannia and Gordon's Rock. Abraham Gabemma, a pioneer explorer, came across this beautiful valley in 1657. It is said that when he saw the sun glittering on the nearest dome-shaped boulder it seemed to him like a huge pearl, and it is from this that Paarl derives its name. It was not until 1687 that the first few settlers from the Cape came to the valley, and a year later they were joined by a number of refugee French Huguenot families.' The traffic started to move, and from the back of the coach Luke Tanner applauded her silently in a way that distracted her momentarily. She felt herself blush for the second time in some years, and she turned her back on the passengers for a brief moment to regain her composure. Bill took the coach forward slowly, but they stopped again to let vehicles through from the opposite side. Amy at last got a grip on herself to continue speaking. 'I might also take this opportunity to mention that we shall be stopping for lunch at Franschhoek, and you will have time to visit the Huguenot Memorial and the Saasveld Museum where they have records on display of the French Huguenot families who originally settled in this valley.'

A traffic policeman waved his arms, indicating that Bill could take the coach through the gap they had cleared, and the passengers cheered and clapped as the coach picked up speed towards their planned destination.

What was Luke Tanner doing on this tour? Surely he had more important things to do? His presence unsettled her and made her feel as if she was under surveillance to ascertain whether she was doing her work properly. She could feel that unfamiliar anger rising inside her again, but she suppressed it forcibly as Bill took the turn-off towards their first port of call.

There were vineyards now to the left and the right of the coach, and Amy rose once again to unhook the microphone. She turned to face the passengers, her glance carefully avoiding the man seated at the back, and the faint crackling sound could be heard in the coach as she flicked the switch.

'We are paying a visit to the Bordeaux estate this morning, and it lies south-east of Paarl, between the Paarl and Klein Drakenstein mountains.' Amy's pleasant voice carried across the speakers. 'The present owner of Bordeaux is Dirk du Bois, and the estate has been in the du Bois family for more than a century. The original homestead still exists, but it now consists of offices for the staff, and a spacious tasting-room where you may sample the excellence of Bordeaux wine while you are shown a video of the entire procedure from the harvesting of the grapes to the bottling of the wine.'

The coach slowed down as they approached the impressively arched stone entrance to Bordeaux. Beyond it lay the vineyards, the vines cut down severely to await the new growth, and from those vines would come superb quality wines such as Cabernet Sauvignon, Pinotage, Riesling, Columbard and Steen. The coach moved slowly up the treelined avenue towards the gabled buildings. To the left lay the present home of Dirk and Alison du Bois, attractively situated among old oaks with gnarled trunks which cast a welcome shade across the spacious garden. It was, however, towards the original homestead on the right that Bill steered the coach, and Amy could see Connie Hayward and Myrna Cawley waiting to welcome the visitors to Bordeaux.

Bill parked the coach in a shady spot where it would remain until their departure, and Amy once again flicked the switch on the microphone.

'Your guide on this tour will be Connie Hayward, and afterwards she will be only too happy to answer whatever queries you may still have.' Amy consulted her wrist-watch. 'The coach will depart from Bordeaux at twelve noon, which is in two hours' time, and I must ask you all please not to be late as we're running to a tight schedule this morning. Thank you.'

Bill opened the doors as she returned the microphone to its resting place, and Amy led the way out of the coach towards the two young women dressed in neat blue skirts and white blouses.

'Hello, Connie,' she smiled at the dark-haired girl who came forward to meet her. 'I have twenty-seven for you today.'

'I think we'll have to split them into two groups,' Connie Hayward decided, her glance darting towards Myrna Cawley for confirmation. 'I'll take one group, and Myrna can take the other, but don't worry, Amy, I'll sort them out.'

'Thanks,' Amy murmured, glancing nervously

over her shoulder just as Luke Tanner stepped
down from the coach.

'Ladies and gentlemen, will you come this way,
please?' Connie instructed, stepping forward to
organise the group of tourists while Amy walked
quickly towards the office. 'We don't usually receive
such a large group of visitors at once, so we're going
to split you into two groups, but first I'd like you to
accompany me to the tasting-room where you may
sample a glass of Bordeaux-estate wine while you
watch the video we have set up for you. After that
we'll be visiting the winery and the cellars.'

Amy stepped into the cool foyer of the old
building where the girls had their offices, and
Jessie Milford's hazel eyes smiled up at her as she
approached the desk. 'We have twenty-seven
visitors for the tasting-room today, Jessie.'

'The tourist business is certainly looking up,'
Jessie grinned. 'I'd better go and make sure that
there are enough chairs and glasses.'

Amy felt a prickly sensation coursing up her
spine and she turned abruptly to see Luke Tanner
entering the small foyer with his jacket hooked on
a finger over one broad shoulder.

'Why aren't you with the rest of the group?' she
demanded sharply, her nerves reacting violently to
his disturbing presence.

'I've visited Bordeaux several times before.' He
stunned her into silence with this information,
then his tawny glance went beyond her to the girl
who had risen behind the desk. 'Hello, Jessie.'

'Good morning, Mr Tanner,' Amy heard Jessie
greet him in a voice which was suddenly
breathless.

'Is Dirk in the cellars?' Luke questioned the girl
while Amy stood immobile and rendered momentarily speechless.

If Luke Tanner was acquainted with the du Bois family, then what was he doing on this tour? Amy knew the answer to that question, but until that moment she had stubbornly ignored it. He was there because of her, and it frightened rather than flattered her.

'Mr du Bois was here a moment ago on his way to the vineyards,' Jessie informed Luke. 'You'll find Mrs du Bois at the house, though, and I'm sure she'd be glad to see you.'

'Thank you.' A strong had gripped Amy's arm, and she felt again that twitching of her nerves as if she had come into contact with a live current. 'Come along, Amy, I'll introduce you to Alison du Bois.'

'I've met her in the course of duty,' Amy found her voice at last while she was being marched out of the office. 'Bringing tourists here to Bordeaux doesn't give me the right to fraternise with the owners, and I doubt that Mrs du Bois will look kindly upon the breaking of that rule.'

'Don't be ridiculous!' Luke laughed shortly, his fingers tightening on her arm when she tried to free herself. 'Alison is a warm, sensitive and intelligent woman, and she loves receiving visitors.'

They walked round to the front of the gabled homestead, and up the steps towards the large, ornately carved door with its heavy brass knocker gleamed in the sunlight. Luke raised the knocker and brought it down twice, sharply. There was a lazy smile in those heavy-lidded eyes as he looked down at her from his great height, but Amy suddenly felt as if her features had been carved of stone. Why was she letting this man take charge of her in this way as if she did not have a will of her own?

The door opened, and Amy found herself

B

staring nervously at the woman standing there.
Alison du Bois was slightly taller than Amy; her
dark brown hair had a hint of copper in its sheen
as she stood in the shaft of sunlight entering the
house through the open door, and her lovely
features broke into a smile that sparkled in her
lively grey-green eyes.

'Luke!' she exclaimed in a faintly husky voice as
she stepped forward and reached up to kiss him on
the cheek. 'How marvellous to see you!'

Her welcome was warm and friendly, and Amy
judged Alison du Bois' age to be the same as her
own when she suddenly found those smiling grey-
green eyes looking directly into her own.

'I believe you've met Amy Warren,' Luke
remarked, releasing Amy's arm and affording her
a certain amount of relief.

'Yes,' Alison acknowledged without the slightest
indication that she was curious or surprised to see
Amy there with Luke. 'Hello, Amy,' she said with
that friendly warmth in her husky voice, 'and do
come in, both of you.'

The hallway was enormous, with magnificent
chandeliers hanging from the high ceiling and
ancient tapestries on the walls. Amy caught her
breath in appreciation as they followed Alison into
the living-room with its attractive mixture of old
and new furniture.

'I hope you don't mind, but Mr Tanner insisted
that I accompany him,' Amy attempted to
apologise for her presence.

'I don't mind at all,' Alison assured her with
that warm smile. 'Salome will be bringing in the
tea at any moment, and do forgive the toys
scattered across the living-room carpet, but Julia is
in one of her impossible moods this morning.'

Her remark drew Amy's attention to the little

girl who was pulling herself up against a chair. She could not have been more than a year old, with golden-blonde curls framing the rounded face with the wide blue eyes, and from the shadows of the past came the memory of a pain best forgotten.

'Hello, there, young Julia,' Luke smiled, flinging his jacket on to a chair, and bending down to pick up the child. 'Your mother says you're being impossible this morning.'

Julia gurgled and smiled, pearly-white teeth appearing between her parted pink lips, and her chubby hands touched Luke's cheeks as if she was actually glad to see him. She chattered away in baby talk, and Luke nodded gravely as if he understood perfectly.

'She doesn't agree with you, Alison,' he said at length to the slender woman who was retrieving the toys and dropping them into a box.

'She never does, the little rascal,' Alison laughed with a wry humour. 'She takes after her father, but that isn't such a bad thing either, and . . . ah, here comes the tea.' A big, buxom, coloured woman in a blue overall entered the living-room with a tray of tea and placed it on the low table close to the sofa. 'Thank you, Salome.'

'Shall I take *kleinmies* Julie?' the woman asked, smiling and bobbing a curtsy of recognition at Luke who was still amusing the child.

'Yes please, Salome,' Alison nodded.

Julia went quite happily from Luke's arms into Salome's, and Alison indicated that Amy and Luke should make themselves comfortable while she seated herself behind the tray and poured tea into delicate china cups.

'Now,' Alison began, smiling across at Luke when they sat drinking their tea and nibbling at home-baked biscuits, 'it's been months since the last time we saw you, Luke, so tell me all your news.'

Amy listened in silence and with growing admiration while Luke explained the success of a business venture which had still been in the incubation stage at their last meeting. He spoke with a lack of affectation, but Amy realised that he possessed a keen, exceedingly clever mind, and her respect for him grew rapidly.

Alison had responded to Luke's information with a knowledge that had astounded Amy, but there was a mischievous smile on Alison's features when she prompted, 'What news do you have for me on the personal front?'

'What news do you expect to hear, Alison?' Luke counter-questioned with that lazy smile in his tawny eyes.

'After you celebrated your thirty-eighth birthday I imagined you would make a more concerted attempt to find yourself a good wife who would give you a few heirs to inherit your empire one day.' Alison announced her expectations quite bluntly. 'There hasn't been a shortage of women in your life, so what's preventing you from taking that final step?'

'I'm not in the market for marriage,' Luke answered with equal bluntness. 'It's a commitment that doesn't appeal to me, and I doubt if it ever will.'

On that particular subject we agree perfectly, the thought flashed through Amy's mind, but there was a difference. She wanted no commitment of whatever nature.

'The trouble with you, Luke, is that you have a way with women,' Alison rebuked him with a hint of amusement in her grey-green eyes. 'And women tend to give you whatever you want with no strings attached.'

'That's the way I like it.' His gaze settled on Amy with a suddenness that made her heart leap into her throat. 'Variety adds spice to life, and changing my women periodically certainly makes my life more interesting and exciting.'

Amy felt as if she was being summed up as a possible candidate, and her face grew warm beneath his prolonged, probing glance.

'Oh, I give up,' Alison laughed, easing the tension and capturing Amy's attention. 'How many people on your tour this morning, Amy?'

'Twenty-seven with Mr Tanner,' Amy announced, swallowing down her last mouthful of tea to hide her confusion.

'Since when do you need to visit Bordeaux with a tour group, Luke?' Alison demanded indignantly.

'I'm investigating the possibility of a future transaction.'

His gaze returned to Amy, and she found herself toying with the crazy notion that the transaction he was referring to was something personal between Luke and herself rather than a business transaction.

Alison du Bois obviously thought the same. Her glance was suddenly intensely curious as it went from one to the other, and her mouth formed a faintly dismayed circle as she murmured, 'Oh?'

She appeared to be waiting for an explanation, but Luke rose calmly to his feet and picked up the jacket he had discarded earlier. 'I think I'll go down to the vineyards to have a few words with Dirk.'

'Take the Land Rover parked outside, Luke,' Alison suggested, 'and you'll find the keys on the stand in the hall.'

'Thanks.' He raised a hand in salute, and his

glance included both Alison and Amy. 'See you later.'

He closed the door behind him as he left the house, and seconds later they heard the Land Rover driving away. The atmosphere in the living-room was suddenly awkward, and Amy was on the point of excusing herself when Alison asked quietly, 'How long have you known Luke?'

'We met for the first time last Friday,' Amy answered, placing her cup on the tray and brushing imaginary crumbs off her skirt to hide her nervousness.

'I have a feeling that somehow, between Luke and myself, we have embarrassed you abominably.'

The unmistakable apology in her warm, husky voice startled Amy. 'You haven't embarrassed me, Mrs du Bois.'

'Alison . . . please,' she corrected.

'It was very kind of you to invite me into your home, Alison, and I don't doubt that it was on the strength of your friendship with Luke.' Amy felt her tense muscles relax slightly. 'If I have felt embarrassed, then it's simply because Mr Tanner appears to take a delight in making me feel that way.'

'Luke can be a tease,' Alison admitted, 'but you'll like him once you get to know him better.'

'I don't dislike him, but neither do I have the desire to get to know him better,' Amy voiced her feelings in no uncertain terms.

'Luke has that same determined look about him that I once encountered in my husband, and I don't think you're going to be allowed a choice of whether you do or don't want to get to know him.' Alison du Bois had a distant, faintly amused look in her eyes. 'Luke can be very obstinate and sometimes ruthless when he wants something, and I've seen many women succumb to his particular brand of charm, but I suspect he's not going to find it quite so easy with you.'

Alison du Bois was a shrewd judge of character, and for some strange reason Amy felt that this woman understood her predicament without having to be told.

They talked for a while longer, and Amy discovered that Alison and Dirk du Bois also had a five-year-old son, Ferdie, who doted on his father, adored his mother, and spoiled his little sister. Amy felt a tug of envy. She had once been part of such a close-knit family, but from a very early age her life had been dogged with disaster.

Amy channelled her thoughts swiftly back into the present and glanced at her wrist-watch. 'I really must go.'

'There's a little matter I still have to set straight,' Alison smiled as she walked Amy to the door. 'You said earlier that I had invited you into my home on the strength of our friendship with Luke, and there may have been a dash of truth in that, but now that I have had the opportunity to become acquainted with you I would like you to feel free to drop in again.'

There was complete sincerity in the eyes that met Amy's, and an answering smile curved her sensitive mouth. 'You're very kind, Alison, and I must thank you for the lovely tea.'

It was three minutes to twelve and Amy was chatting to Myrna Cawley. She had checked the passengers on the coach and the only one not present was Luke Tanner. If there was a delay because of him she would be furious, but the thought had barely skipped through her mind when a Land Rover sped towards the coach and skidded to a halt in a cloud of dust. A dark-haired little boy was on the back seat of the vehicle, and the man behind the wheel was unmistakably Dirk du Bois, but he was not looking in Amy's direction. He was saying something to Luke Tanner, who was getting out on the passenger side of the Land Rover, to which Luke responded, 'I'll keep that in mind,' as he stepped aside and raised his hand in salute.

Dirk du Bois pulled away at the same speed at which he had stopped, but for one brief second his grey eyes met Amy's with a hint of curiosity and amusement in their depths that a sent a surge of heat into Amy's face. Dammit, she was blushing like a schoolgirl lately, and it was an uncomfortable feeling.

'Am I late?' Luke asked, striding towards her with that air of confidence possessed mainly by men of importance such as himself and, against her will, Amy experienced a sense of awe.

'Another minute and you would have been late,' she said, glancing at her watch and, taking her leave of Myrna, she preceded Luke into the coach.

The tour continued to Franschhoek, a picturesque little town surrounded by orchards and vineyards, nestling at the foot of the Franschhoek mountains. They stopped for lunch at a restaurant in the town, and the visitors seated themselves at tables with red checked tablecloths while Amy confirmed the arrangements with the manager.

She did not see Luke enter the restaurant, but when she sat down at her usual table close to the door, it was Luke who sat facing her across the checked tablecloth, and not Bill.

'Your driver agreed to exchange places with me.' Luke answered her query before she could put it into words. 'You don't mind, do you?'

'I doubt if it would matter to you if I did,' she countered icily, her eyes darkening with an anger she was having difficulty in controlling. 'There is one thing, however, which I feel you ought to remember. You may have it within your power to manipulate most people you come into contact with, but I don't take kindly to that sort of treatment, and most especially not when it disrupts the routine of my job.'

'I'm impressed,' Luke mocked her. 'As a matter of fact you have impressed me all morning, and I must congratulate you on the skilful way you've conducted this tour. I'm now all the more determined to put my plan into action.'

'What is that supposed to mean?' she demanded coldly, her angry, unwavering glance meeting his across the small table.

'I have a proposition I want to put forward to your uncle and, if he accepts it, I might well be in a position to manipulate your life during the coming weeks and months.'

His smile was enigmatic, but there was a steely quality about him that injected ice into her veins. Luke Tanner was not a man to be trifled with, Amy realised. His raw masculinity could quicken the pulse, his sensuality and charm could weaken a woman's resolve as well as her knees, but if he was crossed in business he would be a deadly opponent. She was not unaware of the power he wielded, and she also knew that she would have no weapon with which to fight him if he should transfer that power to a personal level.

'What is it that you don't like?' he interrupted her thoughts. 'Is it the thought of a business deal between Aloe Tours and myself, or is your dislike personal?'

His bluntness was disconcerting, but she parried

it with a query of her own. 'Why this sudden interest in Aloe Tours, Luke?'

His name had slipped out before she could prevent it, and her startled expression brought a mocking smile to his lips. 'I like the way you say my name.'

'Don't change the subject!' she snapped, a touch of pink spreading across her cheekbones.

'Very well,' he drawled. 'The economic recession is making most companies feel the pinch, and it's pushing some into the red. When an opportunity comes along you take it, and that's what I'm doing.' He removed his arms from the table and leaned back in his chair to make room for their lunch which was being served, but the moment they were alone again he said, 'Now it's your turn to answer *my* question.'

Amy stared down at her plate of food. How could she answer him without making him realise that as a man he had such a devastating effect on her that she would have preferred it if they had never met in the first place? How could she explain that his presence made her feel as if her calm, orderly life was in the process of being disrupted?

'I've told you before that I don't dislike you,' she said lamely, sampling her food as a legitimate excuse to avoid his probing glance.

'Am I to understand, then, that you dislike the idea of a business deal between Aloe Tours and my company?'

She looked up quickly, her startled eyes meeting his, and she hastily swallowed the food in her mouth. 'No, that isn't true!'

'What is the truth, then?'

'Eat your *bobotie*, it's delicious.' She wriggled herself out of that tight corner, but there was something in his tawny eyes that led her to believe she would not always succeed so easily.

'You're like a puzzle with several pieces missing,' he said, studying her intently through narrowed eyes, 'but I'm going to make it my business to find those missing pieces, Amy.'

Her eyes had become two dark pools in a face that had gone white. She did not want anyone prying into her life, least of all Luke Tanner, and she did not want that hidden part of her exposed and dissected by someone who could not possibly understand. She was aware of Luke's glance resting on her pale features, but he did not question her, and neither had she any intention of explaining.

They ate their lunch and drank their tea in comparative silence, but the tourists were in a jovial mood and eager to continue the tour when it was time to leave the restaurant.

After a brief stop at the Huguenot Memorial they went on to Solitaire, one of the two estates owned by Kate and Rhyno van der Bijl. Solitaire did not have all the facilities for tourists which Bordeaux offered, but the wines produced from this estate were known throughout the country, winning European acclaim as well, and the visitors had the opportunity to sample and buy Solitaire wine direct from the estate.

The trip back to Cape Town always seemed to take less time than the trip out, but on this occasion Amy was so occupied with her own troubled thoughts that they appeared to arrive in the 'Mother City' in record time. The tourists thanked Amy for a delightful trip when they arrived at the terminal, Bill received a substantial gratuity as their driver, and soon they dispersed leaving only Luke Tanner.

'Do you have to go to your office, or do you go straight home from here?' he asked, putting on his jacket and glancing at his watch.

'I have to call in at the office.'

'Do you need a lift?'

'No, thanks,' she declined abruptly. 'I have my car.'

'Then all that remains is for me to thank you for a very pleasant day,' he smiled faintly. 'We'll meet again, Amy, and this time quite soon.'

She stood there watching him walk away from her, and she was aware suddenly that she was shaking like a leaf. It was relief after a particularly gruelling day in his presence, she told herself, but there was a part of her that suggested it was a fear of something yet to come.

CHAPTER THREE

THE telephone had been ringing non-stop that Wednesday morning, and Amy's cup of tea had gone cold before she could touch it. She was contemplating asking Penny to make her a fresh cup when the interleading door opened and Uncle Ben walked in. He was excited about something— she could see it in his eyes—and she did not have long to wait to find out what it was he had on his mind.

'Luke has made us an offer we would be foolish to refuse, and I want you to drop everything and go along to Tanner House,' he said, gesturing her to silence when she would have interrupted him. 'Luke will explain everything, and the details can be thrashed out between the two of you.'

Amy was not in the mood for Luke Tanner. She had had a bad night after yesterday's trip into the winelands, and her temper was beginning to show visible signs of erupting.

'Wouldn't it be wiser for you to see Luke, Uncle Ben?'

'You're quite capable of handling this, so don't be difficult, Amy.'

'I'm not trying to be difficult,' she protested heatedly, 'but the less I see of Luke Tanner, the better I like it.'

'Why?'

Why? There were several answers she could have given, but her uncle would not have understood one of them. 'Let's just say we rub each other up the wrong way.'

'Fiddlesticks!' Her uncle brushed aside her explanation. 'You'll handle this transaction far better than I can, so get going.'

Her dark eyes widened with a mixture of dismay and anger. 'You mean I'm to go and see him immediately?'

'At once!' Ben stressed the urgency. 'Luke is expecting you so I suggest you don't waste any time.'

'So, Luke Tanner snaps his fingers and everyone has to jump!' she exploded. 'Very well, Uncle Ben, I'll go, but I don't like the idea, and you might as well know it.'

She threw a notebook and pen into her briefcase, checked her make-up, and stormed out of the office, leaving her uncle and Penny staring after her with curious, slightly bewildered expressions on their faces.

Tanner House was on the foreshore of Cape Town. It was a magnificent, modern, ten-storeyed building with an ornamental garden at the entrance, and a car park at the side for visitors. Amy had seen it often from the outside, never dreaming she would ever have cause to enter it, but she was too angry to be impressed when the glass doors opened automatically for her to enter the air-conditioned foyer with its Italian tiles on the floor and potted palms.

A security officer behind a counter asked her name and enquired after her business. She penned her name in the book he pushed towards her, and a visitor's tag was clipped to the wide collar of her cinnamon-coloured dress. The security doors slid open to admit her, and she was instructed to take the lift up to the ninth floor.

Amy's anger wavered in the lift that swept her up to the floor on which Luke had his offices, and a nervous flutter erupted at the pit of her stomach. She would be meeting Luke for the first time in his own private domain, and she was not sure what to expect. The lift doors parted silently and she stepped out into a carpeted foyer smaller than the one on the ground floor.

A pretty blonde looked up as Amy approached her desk and smiled a welcome. 'Your name, please?'

'Amy Warren.'

The girl flicked a switch beneath her desk and glass doors opened behind her. 'Mr Tanner's office is down the passage to your right.'

Amy was by now sufficiently impressed, and those nervous flutters in her stomach were increasing rapidly. The carpeted floor muted her footsteps as she walked towards a door that stood open, and as she neared it she could hear the sound of a word processor in use. Her heart was hammering in her throat when she entered the office with its modern steel furniture and, when Luke's attractive, dark-haired secretary asked if she was Amy Warren, Amy nodded mutely.

'You may go through,' the woman announced, her green gaze speculative as she indicated the panelled door. 'Mr Tanner is expecting you.'

'This is ridiculous! Pull yourself together, Amy Warren!' Amy rebuked herself fiercely and, squaring her shoulders, she tapped lightly on the door, opened it, and stepped inside.

The office was furnished in warm autumn shades with comfortable leather armchairs at one end, but Amy's glance was drawn towards the opposite end of the room where Luke Tanner stood up behind the enormous mahogany desk. His dark grey suit was immaculate and expensive, accentuating the width of his shoulders and the

leanness of his hips, but it was the lazy smile in his
tawny eyes that captured and held her glance.

'Close the door, Amy, and sit down.' He
gestured towards the chair on the opposite side of
his desk, and she was annoyed with herself when
she felt her legs shaking beneath her as she did as
she was told. A tray of tea stood on his desk, and
that lazy smile was still in his appraising eyes when
he said, 'May I offer you a cup of tea, or would
you prefer something stronger?'

Her nervousness evaporated and her anger
returned when she encountered his uncanny ability
to gauge her feelings. He knew she was nervous,
and he might have been teasing with his reference
to 'something stronger', but in her present frame
of mind it sounded as if he were laughing at her.

'Tea will do, thank you,' she answered coldly,
placing her shoulder bag next to her briefcase on
the carpeted floor at her feet.

Luke sat down behind his desk, asked her how
she liked her tea, and poured it with a deftness she
did not expect from someone like him. He leaned
across to place her cup of tea in front of her, and
her glance was trapped in his gaze.

'You didn't want to come here, did you?'

His statement jolted her, but there was no sense
in denying the truth. 'No, I didn't.'

'I admire honesty.' Luke's smile deepened
sensuously. 'When honesty in a woman is coupled
with beauty I find the attraction doubly strong.'

Amy stiffened beneath the blatant intimacy of
his appraisal. 'If we're to do business together,
then I suggest we leave personal feelings out of it.'

'Those are my sentiments exactly, but I think
you're the one who is having difficulty in applying
that rule.'

The truth was like a glass of icy water being

dashed in her face, making her realise that she had made no attempt to hide her displeasure at having to confront him on a business level. She had, to date, come close to being abominably rude to this man, and the blame was hers entirely for allowing him to affect her in such a physical way.

'I'm sorry,' she murmured ruefully, lowering her long, dark lashes and staring at her hands locked so tightly together in her lap.

'You're forgiven,' he said with a smile in his voice. 'Drink your tea, then we'll talk business.'

The tea was warm and strong, and it steadied her nerves considerably. Her composure slipped much too easily in this man's company, and she had to take a firmer grip on herself if she did not want to succumb to his fatal charm and magnetism.

'What is it that you have in mind, Luke?' she asked when they had finished their tea.

'There are Blue Dolphin hotels all along the coast from here to Durban and further inland.' He was not being ostentatious, just stating a fact, as he lit a cigarette, the smoke curling from his nostrils as he leaned back comfortably in his high-backed chair. 'If your company will organise the coach tours, then I'll be prepared to offer the tourists accommodation at cut-rate prices.'

This was something that Amy had dreamed of for quite some time, but being confronted with the possibility that her dream could become a reality was almost too good to be true. 'I gather you're talking about organised, all-inclusive tours to the various places of interest between Cape Town and Durban?'

'That's correct.' His eyes were narrowed as he studied her through a screen of smoke. 'Do you think Aloe Tours is capable of coping with an assignment such as that?'

'We'll cope,' she said with conviction and growing excitement.

'That's what I thought when I watched you in action on the tour yesterday,' he smiled faintly. 'How long would it take to get the project off the ground?'

Amy made a swift mental calculation. 'Three months, perhaps.'

'Make it two.' Luke put on the pressure. 'We're losing out on October, but if we could have these tours functioning from November through to March this season, then it would still be worthwhile.'

'In that case we'd better get down to discussing the details.' Amy lifted her briefcase on to her lap and opened it to take out her notebook and pen. 'I shall need a list of the hotels you're making available to us, and I shall have to know what tariff you have in mind.'

'I have that information right here,' he said, opening a brown folder on his desk and taking out several typed sheets which he passed to her across the desk.

Amy studied the list and found the tariffs more reasonable than she had expected. Her mind was leaping ahead, making plans and calculating costs, but she had to take Luke Tanner into consideration.

'Did you have anything specific in mind for these tours?' she asked politely, and his strongly chiselled mouth curved in a smile that did something extraordinary to her pulse rate.

'You're the expert in this field,' he said soberly. 'I'll leave the organising of the tours in your capable hands, but on the understanding that I'd like to be kept up to date with the details of the progress you're making.'

'There's a lot of ground work to cover before we can actually set the wheels in motion,' she warned. 'For a start I shall have to visit your hotels for a detailed description of the accommodation you have to offer, and photographs will have to be taken for the brochures to advertise the tours.'

Luke nodded, drawing hard on his cigarette and crushing the remainder into the marble ashtray on his desk. 'That can be arranged whenever you're ready.'

'We'll also need to have a contract drawn up,' she pointed out, her eyes on those strong, slender-fingered hands laced together on his desk blotter.

They were nice hands: a lover's hands. A wave of heat surged through her. God, what was she thinking about!

'My lawyer will be in consultation with yours to draw up a contract which will be satisfactory to both parties.' That deep, baritone voice intruded on the erotic and totally alien thoughts skipping through her mind, and she pulled herself together with an angry effort.

The time seemed to fly while they discussed the project, and when she finally glanced at her watch she was surprised to discover that it was a quarter to one. 'Well, I don't think we have anything more to discuss until I've drawn up a rough draft of what I envisage.'

'It's time for lunch, wouldn't you say?' Luke smiled, getting up behind his desk and walking round to her side as she snapped shut her briefcase and picked up her handbag. 'I've booked us a table at a quiet restaurant not far from here.'

Amy rose to her feet and hid her feelings behind a cool mask when she found herself looking a long way up into his rugged face. 'I don't recall that I agreed to have lunch with you.'

'I never asked, I simply assumed that you would, and I know that you're not going to disappoint me,' he announced with infuriating arrogance, as he took her arm and escorted her out of his office through a door that led directly into the passage. 'We do have something to celebrate, don't we?' he asked, thumbing the lift button.

'I would say that a celebration at this stage is much too premature,' she argued coldly.

'I don't agree with you, Amy,' he contradicted her as the lift doors slid open and they stepped into it. 'I have the greatest faith in your ability to make a success of this venture.'

'I've heard all about psychological stimuli,' she could not help smiling, '. . . that you should use praise lavishly if you want a little more than the best from someone doing a job for you.'

He laughed throatily as the lift swept them down to the ground floor and the pleasant sound of his laughter seemed to envelop her in the confined space. 'I can't fool you, can I?'

'Not one bit,' she assured him.

He grimaced slightly and issued a belated invitation. 'Will you have lunch with me?'

'You have already booked a table, haven't you?'

Her smile had deepened with a hint of mockery until the corners of her soft, pink mouth dimpled. A strange look entered Luke's eyes as his glance lingered on her mouth, and it was as if she had access to his mind for a brief moment. He wanted to kiss her, and for one crazy moment she wanted it too. What has happened to her? she wondered as she felt the first stirrings of alarm, then the lift stopped and the doors opened.

Relief washed over her at the knowledge that she had been saved from making a fool of herself, but her heart was drumming against her temples and her knees felt weak beneath her when they walked out of the lift towards the security counter. Amy unclipped the visitor's tag with trembling fingers and handed it in, and there was a brief exchange of pleasantries between Luke and the security officer before the glass doors opened to let them through into the foyer.

The luxury and comfort of Luke's red Ferrari was an experience Amy would not have wanted to miss. The front seats could be adjusted for height, thigh, and lumbar support and, coupled with the powerful engine beneath the gleaming bonnet, it felt as if she was floating the short distance to the restaurant he had mentioned.

Luke had been right. The atmosphere at the seafood restaurant was quiet and restful despite the fact that almost all the tables were occupied. The décor gave Amy the sensation of being on an old galleon at sea which added something extra to the enchanting atmosphere.

'Tell me about yourself, Amy.' Luke steered the conversation along a more personal avenue when they had eaten their crayfish salad and were drinking their coffee.

'There's nothing to tell,' she shied away from the subject, but Luke had a determined look about him that placed her on her guard.

'You're a beautiful woman, and you're . . . how old?'

'It's impolite to ask a woman her age,' she pointed out with a smile she could not suppress, but she nevertheless relented. 'I'm twenty-six.'

He studied her thoughtfully, then he shook his head as if he was confused. 'I don't get the impression that you're a dedicated career woman, so how have you managed to stay single?'

'I'm not interested in marriage,' she stated bluntly, and his heavy eyebrows rose in sardonic humour.

'You agree, then, with my philosophy that variety adds spice to life?' he questioned, and her eyes sparkled with amusement when they met his over the rim of her cup.

'Is that a nice way of asking me whether I prefer having brief affairs with men rather than committing myself to the bondage of marriage?'

'Do you?'

There was no humour in his eyes this time as he observed her intently. He was suddenly deadly earnest, and she shook her head, murmuring an abrupt, 'No.'

'I didn't think so,' he smiled slowly, but that smile was gone again the next instant. 'Why do you attempt to freeze men out of your life?'

He was delving too deeply, and she did not like it. 'I don't want to become emotionally or physically involved with a man.'

Her voice was cold to match her expression, but Luke Tanner was not a man to be put off so easily, and she had a suffocating notion that he would not stop until he knew everything there was to know about her.

'You were hurt once, is that it?'

'Yes, I was,' she admitted, still on safe ground, 'and I don't intend to suffer the same agonies twice.'

He put down his cup and placed his hand over hers where it lay on the table. 'Not all men are cads, Amy.'

His remark startled her, but she could not blame him for his incorrect assumption that she had been treated badly and she could not leave him with that thought in mind.

'He wasn't a cad,' she said quietly, sliding her hand from beneath his when she began to feel again those odd sensations spiralling up her arm. 'Do you mind if we change the subject?'

Luke's silent regard was prolonged and discomfiting, then he said brusquely, 'When may I expect to see a rough draft of your plans for this project?'

'I may have something worked out by Friday afternoon,' she answered in an equally brusque, businesslike voice when she had finished her coffee and pushed her cup aside.

'Good,' he nodded, the light against the panelled wall adding a touch of gold to his tawny hair which was styled close to his proud head. 'May I order you more coffee?'

'No, thank you,' she declined stiffly, glancing at her watch, 'and I really must get back to the office.'

'Let's go, then.'

There was a strained silence between them when he drove her back to Tanner House to collect her car, and she wondered why she had that vague feeling of discontent surging through her. She glanced briefly at Luke's stern, rugged profile, and found herself becoming curious about him in a way she had not about anyone else before. She had her own reasons for not wanting to become involved in marriage again, but what were *his* reasons for shunning it so completely?

Luke saw her to her car and left her with an abrupt goodbye. He was angry, she had felt the vibrations emanating from him, and she wondered why. He had angered her often enough since their first meeting, but for some strange reason she did not want him to be angry with her. This was crazy! Luke was having an effect on her which was undermining all her firm resolutions and it had to stop.

It was now Amy's turn to be angry. She had worked herself up into a furious mood by the time she had walked into her office, and had barely sat down when her uncle put his head round the door.

'Well?' he asked with uncharacteristic abruptness.

'Well, *what*?' she snapped.

'Are we in business?' he laughed at her aggression.

'I'm working on something.'

'Wonderful!' he beamed at her, then his head disappeared and the door was closed firmly between their offices.

Amy was well prepared when Luke walked into her office the next Friday afternoon. She had worked on this new project every available moment she had had, day and night, and everything was planned almost down to the last detail for Luke's inspection and approval. Amy ordered tea, and Penny could barely take her eyes off Luke when she brought in the tray and placed it on Amy's desk, but Luke gave no indication that he had noticed. Amy could not blame her secretary entirely. Luke's magnificent physique alone was sufficient to attract female attention, but that aura of authority coupled with his virile masculinity was the downfall of most women. Including herself, she could have added, but she refused to admit defeat.

'What have you got for me, Amy?' Luke asked when she had poured their tea.

Amy was having difficulty channelling her concentration in the direction of business, but she passed him a blue file which contained all the information he required to study at his leisure, and then briefly discussed the most important details with him.

'I've mapped out a route from Cape Town to Durban which includes optional tours, and ends with a flight back to Cape Town if the client should wish to return,' Amy pointed out. 'I have also made tentative arrangements for the delivery of two luxury coaches which will enable us to have a coach leaving Cape Town every alternate week.'

'What happens at the conclusion of the tour?' Luke flicked through the papers in the file. 'Does the coach return to Cape Town to pick up the next batch of tourists?'

'An empty coach on the road is an expenditure we try to avoid at all costs. That's the reason for the two coaches, and that's why, in collaboration with our Durban branch, I have also planned the entire tour in reverse, ending in Cape Town with the optional flight back to Durban.'

'That's a brilliant idea,' Luke smiled, studying the file and swallowing a mouthful of tea.

His lightweight beige suit and brown shirt accentuated his tanned fitness, and she found herself wondering how he succeeded in keeping his body in such magnificent shape. He looked up suddenly, his tawny eyes capturing hers with a suspicion of laughter in their depths that made her wonder if he was aware that she had been studying him and, to hide her confusion, she hastily lapsed into speech with her eyes lowered to the blotter on her desk.

'I've been in telephone consultation with the various publicity associations and, taking everything into consideration, I have calculated the cost for a tour of this nature.'

'The fee's reasonable,' he observed when he had

found the page where she had noted down her calculations. 'What happens next?'

'If you're happy with the initial outline, then I have to start gathering detailed material for the brochure to advertise the tour.' Amy paused for a moment, aware of his glance lingering on the high collar of her white blouse. Then his glance dipped lower to where her small, firm breasts jutted against the silky material, and she was appalled when she felt her breasts responding as if he had actually touched her. 'Could you make the necessary arrangements for me to visit your hotels along that route?' She added her hasty query to draw his attention away from the obvious effect his glance had on her treacherous body.

'I can do better than that.' His mouth curved in a lazy, sensuous smile, and his gaze was once again lowered to where her nipples were straining against the confining material. 'I'll take you personally.'

Amy's heart was suddenly beating in her throat. If her body could react in this way simply because he had looked at her, then she was too afraid even to think of what might occur if she had to spend several days alone in his company.

'That won't be necessary, thank you,' she rejected his suggestion politely and firmly, but she discovered that Luke could be equally polite and firm.

'I insist.'

'But this could take anything up to a week!' she protested.

'I know,' he said with a calmness that infuriated her, and his compelling glance held hers while he drank the last of his tea. 'When do you want to leave?'

There was no way she was going to succeed in

dissuading him, she could see it in his eyes and in the rigid set of his strong jaw, and she reluctantly resigned herself to the inevitable, but not without a certain amount of resentment.

'I want to leave as soon as possible,' she answered him in the cool, businesslike voice which was part of the image she would have to project for her own safety.

'What about tomorrow morning?'

Amy considered this for a moment, doing a swift mental calculation of how much time she would need to prepare herself. Then she nodded abruptly. 'Tomorrow morning would be fine.'

'Give me your address,' Luke instructed, taking a small, black notebook out of his jacket pocket, and Amy wondered how many names and addresses of female acquaintances it contained. The thought was distasteful, but she was obliged to add her own name and address to that long list. She watched him jot down the information she had given him and pocket the notebook before he pushed back his chair and rose to his feet. 'I'll pick you up at seven in the morning,' he said, dropping the blue file she had given him into his briefcase, and then he was striding out of her office.

Amy could not recall at what stage she had stood up, but she found herself staring at the door Luke had closed behind him, and clutching rather weakly at her desk for support. She felt as if she was sliding deeper and deeper into a well from which she would never be freed, and her struggles seemed merely to increase her predicament.

Luke's forceful presence seemed to linger in her office for some time after his departure. It made her insides tremble, and she sat down heavily in the chair behind her desk when her legs finally refused to continue carrying her weight.

It took a while to regain her equilibrium before she could buzz Penny, and her secretary was obviously still in a swoon when she entered the office and sat down facing Amy across her desk.

'Isn't Luke Tanner just the best-looking man you've ever seen?' Penny sighed, an ecstatic expression on her face.

'I wouldn't know,' Amy answered abruptly, determined not to commit herself one way or the other.

'I've heard that he's a devil with women, but now that I've seen him in the flesh I can well understand it. He's terribly sexy,' Penny smiled dreamily, emitting a soft purring sound from deep within her throat, 'and those eyes of his are enough to send delicious little shivers through me.'

'Really?' Amy murmured, pretending not to know what her secretary was talking about and hoping to end the topic of conversation right there, but Penny was bubbling over.

'I believe there was a lot of talk some years ago that he was in love with a girl but she married his best friend instead, and there has been speculation ever since that that's the reason he has never married.' Penny paused for a moment, and a frown appeared on her brow. 'I'll tell you something, though. I don't envy the woman who marries him some day.'

'Why do you say that?' Amy asked, her curiosity getting the better of her this time.

'Her time will be fully occupied fighting off all those women who simply can't leave him alone,' Penny explained. 'And, with all those other women around, who says he'll be faithful to his wife?'

That situation was quite unlikely to present itself, Amy decided, taking Luke's aversion to marriage into consideration.

'Penny, I'm going to be away for a couple of days ... possibly a week.' Amy mentioned the reason why she had called her secretary into her office.

'Where are you going?' Penny enquired curiously.

'Luke Tanner is taking me to some of his hotels along the coast between Cape Town and Durban for a detailed description of the accommodation he has to offer tourists.'

'You lucky so-and-so!' Penny sighed, then a mischievous smile creased her face. 'Take my advice, and put a padlock on the door to your heart.'

Amy had put a padlock on her heart a long time ago. There was always the possibility that someone might find the key, but Amy had hidden it so carefully that she doubted if even *she* could find it. Penny's remark did, however, act as a warning, a warning Amy could not ignore. There was a magnetism about Luke which Amy was only too aware of, and if she did not take care it could lead to something which could only result in pain.

'Take a note of the things I want done while I'm away,' Amy said briskly, and for several minutes dictating the instructions succeeded in staving off her troubled thoughts; but still they nagged at her.

Was she not tempting fate by accepting Luke's offer to accompany her personally on this trip? They would be spending every day together for almost a week and, knowing Luke, he would take up her evenings as well. Luke Tanner was a dangerous element which she had never encountered before and if she was not on her guard at all times she could be caught in a trap of her own making.

Amy brushed these thoughts aside for the

moment and walked into her uncle's office to inform him that she would be away for a couple of days. When she returned to her office she became involved in a problem which had arisen early that morning, and it was not until she arrived at her flat that evening that she thought again of the next few days which she would be spending in Luke's company.

It was silly of her to let it trouble her. All she had to do was treat the entire trip in a cool, distant manner, she told herself while she packed her suitcase. She would do nothing to attract his attention in any way, but when she studied the contents of her suitcase she discovered that she had packed only the clothes which she knew made her look her best. She always wore clothes in which she looked and felt good, but she could not argue away that gnawing suspicion that her selection on this occasion had been influenced by a suppressed desire to look good for Luke Tanner.

This is crazy, she told herself, her hands clutching at the suitcase with the intention of dumping everything out on to her bed and starting all over again with a new selection, but for some obscure reason her intention was never carried out.

CHAPTER FOUR

THE doorbell rang at a quarter to seven on Saturday morning, and Amy wiped her hands nervously down the sides of her blue linen slacks as she walked towards the door and opened it. Wide-shouldered and slim-hipped in beige denim slacks and jacket, Luke filled her doorway, and her heart seemed to do an uncomfortable loop in her breast.

'Come in,' she said, avoiding the look in his tawny eyes when they flicked over her. 'You're a bit early.'

'I was hoping you would offer me a cup of coffee before we leave,' he explained as he closed the door behind him and followed her into the small lounge with its pine furniture and bright floral cushions.

Amy gestured towards the tray on the low table in front of the cane bench. 'Help yourself while I make sure I've packed everything I need.'

She left Luke in the lounge and went quickly into her bedroom. She checked the contents of her suitcase and briefcase before fastening the catches, then she slung her camera as well as her handbag over her shoulder and carried her things into the lounge where Luke stood drinking his coffee.

'I have a strange feeling that you expected me to arrive early,' Luke remarked, and Amy straightened with a smile after depositing her luggage close to the door.

'I thought you might,' she said, and his strong mouth relaxed in an answering smile that made

him look almost boyish despite the tiredness
etched in his rugged features.

He worked much too hard, and probably
seldom relaxed. If he did not take care he could
ruin his health, and that would be such a pity.
Good heavens! Amy halted her thoughts abruptly.
I'm beginning to like the man!

'I've been admiring your paintings,' he informed
her, waiting until she was seated with her cup of
coffee before he sat down himself. 'Did you study
art?'

Amy glanced up at the landscapes against the
wall. She had always been fond of sketching, but
painting had formed part of the therapy which had
been prescribed to aid the healing process after
Keith's death.

'I had a few lessons some years ago,' she said
when she realised that he was waiting patiently for
her to answer him. 'It's mainly a hobby which I
don't have much time for these days.'

'That's a pity.' His glance strayed towards the
two landscapes and the one still life which she had
felt were of a reasonable standard. 'They're very
good,' he offered his opinion.

'Thank you,' she smiled, not quite sure whether
he meant it or whether he was merely being kind.

They drank their coffee and Amy took the tray
through to the kitchen. She washed up, dried and
packed everything away, leaving the kitchen tidy
before she returned to the lounge where Luke was
waiting for her.

'Shall we go?' she asked, suddenly nervous to be
alone with him in her flat, and Luke rose at once.

'If you're ready.'

Luke picked up her suitcase and opened the
door. Amy followed him with the rest of her
things, and locked the door firmly behind her.

They were silent in the lift that took them down to the ground floor, and Amy could not overlook the fact that it was sheer nervousness that kept her jaw rigidly clenched until they stepped out of the building into the early morning sunshine, and walked towards a silver-grey Mercedes parked at the kerb.

'What's happened to your Ferrari?' Curiosity loosened her tongue at last while Luke loaded her belongings into the boot.

'The Ferrari may have comfort and speed, but speed is not something everyone can appreciate, and the Mercedes is less conspicuous.'

'I would have thought you would be accustomed to having the attention focused on yourself,' she mocked him lightly as he slammed the boot shut.

'I don't object to having attention focused on myself when it is necessary, but I value my privacy when I can get it.'

Amy considered this when they got into the car and drove away, and she wondered if a man like Luke Tanner ever really succeeded in having much of that privacy he desired. Knowing how much she value her own privacy, she did not envy him the position he held in society at all.

'I assume you don't often have the opportunity to live a life of your own,' she broke the brief silence between them in the car.

'You assume correctly.' His mouth tightened. 'I can get very nasty sometimes when people intrude on my privacy without an invitation.'

'That's one of the disadvantages of being successful, I suppose.'

'You're right about that,' he answered harshly. 'One of the worst disadvantages is never being sure whether people are being nice to you because they like you, or because of what you are.'

c

'How do you cope with that?' she asked, studying his rugged profile with genuine interest in her honey-brown eyes.

'I've become a pretty shrewd judge of character, even if I say so myself, but I've resorted to having people investigated in the past if I have the slightest doubt about my analysis.'

'Have you had me investigated?' she questioned with a mixture of uneasy concern and cynicism.

'I might still do that,' he smiled, his tawny glance meeting hers briefly. 'You've been exactly the opposite to any woman I've ever known. You've been thoroughly nasty to me since the moment we met, and I'm still trying to discover why.'

Amy felt a sudden tightness in her chest, but she made light of the subject. 'I haven't been nasty all the time,' she contradicted him, 'but have you ever considered the possibility that there might be something in you that triggers off the worst in me?'

'I can't say that I've considered that possibility.' He smiled twistedly. 'What is it about me that brings out the negative in you?'

Amy had to think quickly, but the answer was really quite simple. 'I think Alison du Bois put it in a nutshell when she said that you have a way with women that makes them give you whatever you want.'

'If you're trying to tell me that my charm isn't going to work with you, then I shall be quite devastated,' he teased her, but for once she was not disconcerted.

'Every man meets his Waterloo at some time or another.'

'Ah, but I'm not defeated yet, Amy,' he smiled devilishly. 'I still have an ace or two up my sleeve, and I'm going to play them for all I'm worth.'

Amy laughed off his remark, but there was nothing amusing about that gnawing fear that reared its head like an adder inside her. For the first time in her life she had met a man who could demolish her carefully erected barriers, and she knew that if she was not careful she would assist him in carrying out that act of demolition.

Luke turned off the main road into a small, picturesque village nestling in a lush valley, and although Amy was not hungry, they spent the best part of an hour absorbing the peace of their surroundings while they ate breakfast at one of the few tables the restaurant owner had placed outside beneath the trees. Amy felt as if she was out on a picnic instead of a business trip, and she was almost reluctant to leave when they resumed their journey.

They took the route that bypassed Caledon and Swellendam, and several hours passed before they arrived at Mossel Bay and the first of the Blue Dolphin group of hotels.

The hotel was a modern building on the outskirts of the city overlooking the ocean, and with Luke accompanying her Amy had no difficulty in obtaining the information she required. She finally got out her camera in one of the spacious rooms with their bright floral bedspreads matching the curtains at windows that reached almost from the ceiling to the floor. The rooms had all the electrical amenities a tourist could require, and the added luxury of a private bathroom.

'Is this another of your hobbies?' Luke enquired directly behind her, glancing over her shoulder while she attached a wide-angle lens to her camera.

She allowed herself the admission that his masculine cologne was pleasing to the senses. 'It's a hobby for which I have a constant use,' she explained.

'Do you develop your own prints?'

'Yes, I do.' She checked the speed and the aperture. 'That's part of the fun.'

'What else do you do for fun?'

She stiffened as the conversation veered suddenly towards the personal. 'I read, and I listen to music when I have the time.'

'You choose your interests with great care to exclude men, it seems,' he observed drily.

Amy's nerves were beginning to react violently to that masculine frame standing so close to her that she could feel the heat of his body against her back. 'That's the way I like it,' she hid her feelings behind a calm, cool voice as she raised her camera to focus it.

'You can't spend the rest of your life doing that. It's unnatural.'

'You sound as if you've been taking tips from Uncle Ben on "How to lecture Amy",' she remarked wryly, and with some annoyance.

'Perhaps I may succeed where your uncle has failed.' He placed his hand on her shoulder, its weight and warmth penetrating her ivory-coloured blouse, and making her nerves jangle in response. 'Isn't that a fascinating thought?'

'Fascinating,' she agreed sarcastically, thankful that they were alone in the room. His voice was vibrantly low, blatantly sensual, and her body was beginning to react to it as someone starved would react to sustenance offered them. She drew a steadying breath and nudged him gently in the ribs with her elbow. 'Would you please stand aside so that I can get a clear shot of the length of the room?'

'Certainly.' He stepped aside at once, and Amy's

camera clicked away several times before she lowered it and packed it away with the rest of her photographic equipment. 'Lunch?' Luke suggested, glancing at her enquiringly.

'That would be nice,' she nodded.

He took her arm and escorted her out of the room towards the lift in the foyer, and they were whisked up to the fourth floor. Amy glanced up at Luke curiously, wondering where he was taking her, but she received the answer seconds later when he unlocked a door and ushered her into a spacious lounge furnished in cream and gold.

'Welcome to the executive suite,' Luke smiled, and Amy's perfectly arched brows rose a fraction as she took in the elegance of her surroundings.

'I'm impressed.'

He gestured towards a white, panelled door. 'The bathroom is that way through the bedroom if you want to freshen up before lunch.'

Amy's glance took in something else which she had not noticed until that moment. A table had been laid for two close to the window overlooking the ocean.

'We're having lunch here?' she asked abruptly, not quite sure that she liked the idea of being alone with him in the executive suite, and the gleam of mockery in his eyes told her that he knew exactly what she was thinking.

'It's more private, wouldn't you say?'

'I imagine it is,' she agreed and, taking their conversation that morning into consideration, she resigned herself to the fact that she would have to sit through this 'private' lunch with Luke.

She left her camera bag in the lounge and took only her handbag with her as she walked towards the panelled door and pushed it open. The bedroom had been furnished with the same cream and gold elegance of the lounge, and the bathroom was slightly larger than the others she had seen because it had a shower cubicle instead of a shower over the bath.

Amy was suddenly nervous and jumpy. What was she afraid of? she wondered as she washed her hands in the basin and dried them on the snow-white towel. Was she afraid that Luke might walk into the bedroom and pounce on her? No! That was not Luke Tanner's style, she told her image in the mirror above the basin while she touched up her make-up and pulled a comb through her hair. Luke would be more subtle in his conquering of a woman, but his passion would be no less savage. She was horrified at her own thoughts, and she was angry with herself for her idiotic fears when she walked out of the bathroom to join Luke in the lounge.

Their lunch consisted of sliced ham, cold chicken and salads, with a fruit dessert and coffee to follow. Amy had not been very hungry, but the meal was served so attractively that she found herself taking a liberal helping of everything.

'Do you occupy the executive suites when you visit your hotels?' Amy attempted to make light conversation.

'Sometimes, yes,' Luke answered abruptly.

Amy cast a brief glance across the room, and counted ten chairs and five small tables. 'The living area is almost the size of a conference room.'

'That's quite often what it is.'

She raised her startled glance to his. 'Don't you ever go anywhere simply to relax?'

'I don't have much time to relax,' he smiled twistedly.

'What do you do to ease the tension and the strain which must accompany your professional life?'

That was a dangerous question, and it could provoke the wrong kind of answer, but she had asked it in all earnestness.

'I play the occasional round of golf, but I had a gym rigged up at my house a couple of years ago, and I make a point of spending at least an hour there every morning.' He put his plate to one side and helped himself to dessert. 'Physical exertion is a great reliever of tension and stress, I've found.'

'You ought really to take a complete break away from work,' she advised with a growing concern she could not suppress.

'I was thinking of going on a skiing holiday to Switzerland this December.' His tawny glance captured hers. 'What about coming with me?'

Amy almost choked on a mouthful of dessert, but she managed to swallow it before there were any disastrous results. 'Thanks for the invitation, but the answer is no.'

'Pity,' he smiled ironically, his assessing glance bringing a warmth to her cheeks that made her hate herself as well as him at that moment.

The trip to Oudtshoorn took little more than an hour, and it was an enjoyable drive along the scenic Robinson Pass into ostrich country. Amy had always been fascinated by those gigantic birds with their long necks and valuable plumage, and Luke stopped beside a field where they were grazing so that Amy could watch the beautiful courting dance of the male ostrich.

'The female often needs to be courted avidly and constantly before she accepts the male,' Luke explained, and she glimpsed a look in his eyes that made her suspect he was thinking that his avid and constant courting might reap similar results with her.

She felt that telltale warmth sliding into her cheeks and she looked away, telling herself that she was silly to imagine things, but Luke's soft laughter as they drove on seemed to confirm her suspicion.

At the hotel in Oudtshoorn Amy received the same co-operation from the staff as in Mossel Bay. She took the photographs she required, and Luke arranged for her to be driven to the Publicity Association where she spent most of the afternoon gathering the information they could not give her on the telephone. It was five thirty when she arrived back at the hotel, and Luke was in the foyer talking to the manager when she stepped out of the hot sun into the cool interior of the modern building.

Luke came forward at once and took her arm. 'I'll show you up to your room.'

Amy smiled her thanks, and remained silent in the lift taking them up to the third floor. She felt Luke's eyes on her, willing her to look at him, but she kept her glance riveted to the lift doors until they slid open. They turned left into the carpeted passage, and Luke inserted a key into the lock of the door almost at the end of the passage. He pushed the door open, and Amy entered the room ahead of him.

It was a large room furnished in stark white with green, velvety curtains at the window. The bed, however, was the biggest Amy had ever seen. It seemed to dominate the room as well as her mind, and she stared at it for several startled seconds before she realised that Luke was watching her with an odd look in his eyes that made her pulse quicken alarmingly.

'We'll have a splendid view of the Outeniqua mountains in the morning,' Luke announced, walking across the room to look out of the window.

We'll have a splendid view? Her frightened mind latched on to those words. He could not have planned for them to share this room, could he?

He turned at that moment to look at her with a gleam of sardonic amusement in his eyes as if she had spoken her alarming thoughts aloud. 'I'm in the executive suite, which is right next door to the honeymoon suite.'

Amy's confused and startled mind whirled on at a crazy speed before it slowed down and started functioning properly again. 'This is the honeymoon suite?'

'Tantalising thought, isn't it?' he smiled sensuously, walking towards her, and a strange paralysis gripped her when she stood looking up at him with mere inches separating them. He trailed a lazy finger across her cheek and down along her jaw, his touch like fire against her skin, but something in her eyes must have told him of the fear clamouring through her. 'I've ordered dinner for seven o'clock,' he informed her, lowering his hand abruptly, and turning towards the door. 'Come along to my suite when you're ready.'

'Thanks,' she croaked, but she doubted if he had heard her as he strode out of the room and turned right down the passage towards the executive suite.

Amy closed the door hastily. She was shaking with relief and something else she could not define as she leaned against the door for a moment to steady herself before she opened her suitcase and took out her spongebag containing her personal toiletries. She was behaving like a frightened animal, twitching and jumping at every move Luke made, and imagining the worst when nothing was intended. She was an idiot—and it was possible that Luke was beginning to think so too.

She soaked herself in a hot bath, and she felt her tired, tense muscles relaxing for the first time that day. She took her time bathing, and later selected a floral silk dress with long sleeves as the most suitable for dinner that evening with Luke. There was a slight chill in the air, but the silky material was sufficiently warm, and she applied a light film of moisturiser to her face before adding a touch of power and lipstick. She brushed her hair until it shone with the gloss of raven's wing, and slipped her feet into silver sandals. It was almost seven and, dabbing a touch of perfume behind her ears, she left her room and went along to the executive suite.

She felt perfectly calm when she knocked on the door, but her senses were instantly attacked when the door swung open and Luke stood there in dark grey slacks without a shirt.

'Come in, Amy,' he invited, but she stood there staring at his massive, sun-browned chest with the matting of dark hair that trailed down to the belt of his slacks.

'You're not dressed yet,' she accused, her pulse quickening and her senses responding madly in the face of such raw masculinity.

'A mere matter of putting on a shirt,' he pointed out calmly. 'Come in and pour yourself a drink while I finish dressing.'

Amy shrank from the idea. 'I—I think I——'

'Come on,' he laughed, a long, muscular arm reaching out until strong fingers latched on to her wrist. She was pulled inside quickly and the door was closed, but he did not release her wrist as he studied her with a hint of derision in his glance. 'You're not going to tell me that you've never seen a man without a shirt on before, are you?'

'No, but——' The words locked in her throat as

the clean male smell of him stirred her senses unmercifully, and the tips of her fingers tingled with the desire to explore the texture of his skin. Luke raised her hand, and the hair-roughened warmth of his skin was suddenly against her palm. She stood immobile for stunned seconds, aware of the heavy beat of his heart beneath her palm, then she snatched her hand away and snapped, 'Don't do that!'

'Then don't look at me as if you want to touch me.'

His mockery touched her on the raw. It was true! She *had* wanted to touch him, and shame and anger made her turn blindly towards the door.

'I think I'll settle for dinner in the restaurant.'

'Coward!' He stopped her in her tracks before she had gone more than two paces away, and she turned once again to face him with a defiant look in the honey-brown eyes she raised to his.

'Sometimes it's safer being a coward than to end up doing something one might regret.'

'There isn't much fun in always playing safe, Amy.'

'I'm sure that my idea of fun differs vastly from yours,' she argued stiffly, and the smile in his eyes became a lazy, sensuous appraisal.

'Perhaps if you relaxed a little you'd find that there are many ways we would have fun together,' he challenged her, making her aware of the tension that once again held her in its rigid grasp.

She could not accept his challenge, but she knew that she would provoke his mockery if she walked out of his suite, and it was for the latter reason alone that she decided to stay.

'Might I suggest that you put your shirt on before our dinner arrives?' she said, meeting his gaze unflinchingly, and she did not miss the flicker of triumph in his eyes.

'Pour yourself a drink, and make mine a whisky with lots of ice,' he instructed. 'I'll be with you in a minute.'

Left alone, Amy went to the small refrigerator. She poured Luke a whisky, and helped herself to a gin and tonic to settle her nerves. She had suspected that she might encounter difficulties with Luke during this trip but she had not envisaged quite how difficult it was going to be. She swallowed down a mouthful of her drink, and the quivers began to subside as the liquid hit her stomach. Dammit, she would have to get a grip on herself.

Luke emerged from the bedroom a few minutes later. The top buttons of his pale blue shirt had been left undone to expose the tanned column of his strong throat as well as a portion of his chest. Amy's palm still tingled with the remembered texture of his skin. Luke tasted his whisky and turned to face her with a hint of laughter in his eyes as if he had picked up her thought-waves, and she turned away from him before he saw the pink sweeping into her cheeks.

There was a knock on the door, and Luke went to open it. Their dinner was wheeled in on a trolley, the silver salvers gleaming in the light coming from the glass bubbles hanging low from the ceiling.

'We'll help ourselves,' Luke informed the waiter, giving him a substantial tip, and then they were alone once again.

They seated themselves at the table which had been laid for them, and Amy discovered that Luke had ordered creamy asparagus soup, marinated ostrich steaks with fresh vegetables, and an ice-cream dessert with hot chocolate sauce.

The drink and the appetising meal helped to

ease the tension in Amy. Luke was actually a very interesting man to talk to: he had experienced so much, and he had met so many unusual people that she could have listened to him for hours. He was also very much attuned to the basic things in life, but what surprised her most was the discovery that he was a very lonely man with few people whom he could entirely trust. This information had filtered through to her without him actually realising it, but it had changed some of her earlier beliefs about people in his position.

'That meal was superb,' she sighed almost two hours later, dabbing at her mouth with her table napkin when she had finished her coffee.

'What about another drink?' Luke suggested.

'No, thank you,' she declined, pushing back her chair and rising to her feet. 'I must go.'

'It's still early,' he protested.

'This is a business trip, not a holiday,' she reminded him firmly, 'and I have quite a few notes to make before I can think of going to bed.'

'Good heavens, Amy!' His eyes were incredulous as he rose to his feet. 'The night has only just begun and you're actually going to desert me.'

'Oh, I'm sure you'll find something, or someone to amuse you,' she mocked him lightly, and the devilish gleam she had noticed before entered his eyes.

'I was hoping you would do that.'

'Not a chance!' she laughed, turning away from that charm which could so easily prove fatal and walking towards the door. 'Good night, Luke.'

They left Oudtshoorn after breakfast the following morning with the long drive ahead of them to Port Elizabeth. This trip included a brief stop at the seaside resort of Jeffrey's Bay, but the Mercedes was comfortable and air-conditioned and the Garden Route particularly beautiful that year which seemed to make the journey faster on that warm, sunny day.

A strong breeze was blowing when they arrived in Port Elizabeth during the afternoon, and Luke drove directly to the hotel, taking the road along the seafront.

'You've done enough for today,' Luke said when at last they walked into the foyer of the ten-storeyed building. 'You will be shown up to your suite and you're to rest. That's an order. You can attend to everything else in the morning before we leave for East London.'

Amy did not want to argue with him. She was hot and tired and, although he did not show it, she imagined that Luke must feel tired as well.

'Dinner at seven this evening in my suite,' he reminded her, and she nodded, leaving him in the foyer while she followed the porter who was carrying their suitcases towards the lift.

The suite Amy was shown to was more elaborate than the one she had occupied at Oudtshoorn. It had a small private lounge adjoining the bedroom, and the added luxury of a small desk where she could work. She did not want to think of work at that moment and as soon as she was alone she hung out the dress she wanted to wear that evening, stripped down to her panties and bra, and flung herself across the enormous bed.

Amy slept for almost two hours before she was awakened by the sound of someone knocking on her door. She pulled her robe out of her suitcase, putting it on as she went to the door.

'Tea, madam,' the black woman smiled over the tray in her hands.

Amy took the tray from her, thanked her, and pushed the door shut with her hip before she carried the tray across to the low table and chair close to the window. She felt considerably better after the sleep she had had that afternoon and, pouring herself a cup of tea, she sat down and drank it while she stared out across the choppy ocean. After a busy week and all the travelling they had done since the day before, this break of a few hours was exactly what she had needed.

She glanced at her watch. It was after five, but when she had finished her tea she would still have plenty of time to take a leisurely bath before dinner. What was Luke doing? Had he also taken a break, or had he been attending to business all afternoon? Probably not the latter, she decided. Not on a Sunday. Unless, of course, he was a man to whom business meant working a seven-day week. It was really none of her business what he did, she told herself angrily, but she could not help wondering, and she was still thinking about him some time later when she was soaking in a scented bath.

Amy was a little wary of joining Luke for dinner that evening, but unlike the previous evening he was dressed in brown slacks and a shirt when she arrived at his suite, and he behaved impeccably throughout dinner. Their conversation was impersonal, mainly about business, and she found herself relaxing with him, but he got up and barred her way determinedly when she voiced her intention of returning to her own suite.

'You're not going to run away from me again this evening,' he said, taking her arm and leading her out of his suite and into her own. 'Take off your stockings and put on a pair of sandals. It's a warm night now that the wind has died down, and it's ideal for a walk on the beach. Will you come with me?'

The invitation was a mere afterthought. It made her want to laugh, and it also made it difficult for her to refuse.

'All right, I'll go with you,' she smiled up at him and, leaving him in her lounge, she walked into her bedroom to take off her stockings and find a pair of sandals suitable for walking on the beach as he had said.

CHAPTER FIVE

THERE was a refreshing coolness in the night air as Amy and Luke started to walk along the beach. The full moon transformed the ocean into a silver, rippling sheet and added a touch of fluorescence to the foamy breakers rushing up the sandy beach towards them.

Amy drew the salty sea air deep into her lungs, and expelled it in a sigh. 'It's been years since I took a walk along the beach like this.'

'It's something I don't often have the opportunity to do either,' Luke confessed, the deep timbre of his voice blending with the sound of the sea. 'Let's take off our shoes and walk in the shallow water.'

'A good idea,' Amy agreed, pausing to take off her sandals, and waiting while Luke took off his shoes and socks, and rolled his brown cord slacks up to below his knees.

The sand was cool beneath Amy's feet and, carrying their shoes in their hands, they waded ankle deep in the icy water as it washed ashore and drew back again.

'The simple pleasures in life are still the best,' Luke broke the companionable silence between them.

'And the simple pleasures cost nothing,' Amy added.

'Only one's time.'

'And we don't seem to have enough of that these days.'

'I wonder why?'

Amy considered this for a moment before she answered him. 'Perhaps we don't plan our lives well enough to make time for the simple things that give us pleasure.'

'What do you do when you have time away from work?'

'I tidy my flat, do the washing and ironing, and plan what I'm going to do the next day, or the following week.' That sounded dreadfully dull now that she had put it into words. 'What about you?'

'I snatch a moment here and there to read a good book, or I laze around the pool in the sun during the summer.' His stern, rugged profile was etched against the starry sky for a moment, then he turned his head slightly to look at her, and the moon glittered in his tawny eyes. 'If you're Ben's partner in Aloe Tours, then why do you act as a guide on the trip into the winelands?'

'I do it because I enjoy it, and only when there's no one else available.' The tide appeared to be coming in and, looking beyond him, she saw the swell of a foamy breaker less than three metres away from them. She touched his arm to draw his attention to it, and shouted, 'Look out!'

They made a quick dash on to higher ground, but her warning had come too late for both of them. The water had reached up to Amy's knees, wetting the hem of her blue, silk dress, but Luke had been walking nearest the ocean and he was soaked almost to his hips while his shirt had been dampened considerably in the spray. The look that flashed across his face was a mixture of surprise and annoyance, and his dishevelled appearance at that moment was so directly the opposite of the immaculate man she had come to know, that she found herself incapable of suppressing the giggles that rose like a fountain inside her.

Luke raised his head and seemed to glare at her in the moonlight. 'Are you laughing at me, by any chance?'

'I—I can't help it,' she managed, attempting to stifle her giggles and succeeding only partially. 'Your trousers are wet, and so is your shirt,' she stated the obvious.

'Your dress is wet, and I'm not laughing,' he pointed out, making her aware of the damp material clinging about her knees.

'That's because I don't look as silly as you do,' she countered without thinking, but she regretted it the next instant.

'Is that so?' His voice had an ominous ring to it that made her pulses jerk when he stepped up the beach towards her. 'Well, let's see how silly you look when you're as wet as I am.'

'No, Luke, stay away from me!' she warned with a smothered laugh, not wanting the dunking she knew for certain she would get.

'Scared of a little water, are you?' He laughed throatily reaching for her, but Amy had anticipated his move and had turned and fled up the beach at a speed she had not imagined herself capable of.

Their laughter mingled as they raced like children across the sand with Amy in front and Luke coming up at the rear with an agility she had not expected from a man of his size. An involuntary scream passed her lips when Luke's hand gripped her shoulder. She lost her balance as he spun her round, and she collapsed helplessly on to the cool sand at his feet. Luke dropped to his knees in front of her, and they sat there gasping for breath and laughing at each other until their laughter subsided into a silence disturbed only by the sound of the waves crashing on to the deserted shore.

It was years since Amy had felt so carefree and relaxed with anyone, and she found it incredible that it had to happen in the company of a man like Luke Tanner. What was it about this man that he had the power to unleash that part of her which she had thought locked away for ever?

Their eyes met and held in the silvery darkness, and he gently brushed away a strand of dark hair which had blown across her face. His hand lingered against her cool cheek, and she did not flinch away from him when his thumb moved in a light caress across her cheekbone. Amy's heart was still beating hard and fast from the unaccustomed exertion, but suddenly the tempo altered, and she began to sense something in Luke which was finding an echo in her. She tried to curb the feelings sweeping through her, but she might as well have tried to curb the ebb and flow of the ocean. She wanted to touch him, and she wanted to feel that strongly chiselled mouth against her own.

Luke leaned towards her as if she had signalled her desires to him, and his lips brushed lightly against hers at first as if to test her reaction but returned almost instantly for a deeper exploration. She opened her mouth to his, welcoming the intimate invasion of his tongue while her hands unbuttoned his shirt with a near feverish haste to explore the solid warmth of his hair-roughened chest. Luke groaned against her mouth, and his arms were like steel about her, crushing her against his hard body as he eased her down on to the sand and held her there with his weight. His mouth devoured hers, and she responded with a hunger she had had no knowledge of before until the blood soared through her veins, and thudded against her temples to drown out the sound of the ocean.

Beneath the sensual exploration of his hands her body was coming alive in a way which was totally alien to her, and she clung to Luke in a frenzy of desire which was almost frightening in its intensity. The hollows and planes across his broad, muscled back were a delight to explore with her fingertips, but she came to her senses with a stunning force when she felt his heated mouth against the sensitive column of her arched throat before it trailed a devastating path down to the curve of her breast where his fingers had gently brushed aside the silky material.

'No!' she cried out in horror, pushing at him frantically with her hands. 'Oh no, what am I doing!'

He released her at once and she sat up with a jolt, her face ashen in the moonlight. Her fingers were shaking as she tugged at her dress to cover her breasts, and she buried her face in her hands as a wave of shame engulfed her. She was shaking uncontrollably and the storm of feeling he had unleashed in her began to fill her with something close to terror. What on earth had possessed her to allow the situation to develop into something she had almost been incapable of controlling?

'Take it easy, Amy,' Luke spoke calmly, his hands gripping her shoulders. 'This is merely another of those simple pleasures we were discussing earlier.'

'Is that so?' she snapped, brushing aside his hands and leaping to her feet in a fury which was directed mainly at herself. 'Well, it just so happens that it's not quite as simple as that!'

Luke rose slowly, the shirt she had unbuttoned flapping slightly in the breeze, and the sand clinging to his damp trousers, but there was no humour in the situation now as he towered over her with a puzzled expression on his face. 'Don't be afraid of me, Amy. I'll never hurt you.'

'I know!' she answered sharply. 'But that's because I shall never give you the opportunity to do so!'

'Dammit, you're the most confusing woman I have ever met!' he exploded with a harshness that made her flinch inwardly.

They stood glaring at each other in silence for several seconds before Amy calmed herself sufficiently to ask, 'Could we go back to the hotel now?'

His face looked as if it had been carved out of stone when he nodded curtly. They picked up the shoes they had discarded in the confusion, and walked back to the hotel across the sandy beach. Neither of them spoke, and it was difficult to believe that the laughter and the momentary passion had ever occurred between them. It had been a brief madness, and Amy was determined that it would never happen again.

'Good night, Amy,' Luke said when they reached the door to her suite, and his mouth twisted derisively when he added, 'sleep well.'

Amy unlocked the door and went inside. Sleep well, Luke had said, but she had a horrible feeling that she would not sleep at all.

They spent the Monday night at Port St Johns. The atmosphere between them had been strained and tense all day and Amy pleaded a headache that evening to avoid having dinner with Luke. The headache was real enough, it was throbbing against her temples like the pounding of a sledgehammer, and she swallowed a couple of aspirins before taking a relaxing bath and washing her hair.

She had dried her hair and was brushing it vigorously when there was a knock at the door to her suite. Her heart leapt into her throat, and her tired muscles tensed again until they ached.

'Who is it?' she called, her mouth feeling strangely dry.

'Luke,' came the abrupt reply. 'Open up.'

'Just a minute.' She responded to that commanding note in his voice, hastily pulling on her robe over her flimsy nightie before she padded barefoot across the carpeted floor into the small lounge.

She opened the door and her eyes widened at the sight of Luke standing there with a glass of milk and a plate of sandwiches on a tray. Speechless, she stood aside for him to enter, and it was Luke who closed the door behind him before he walked across the room to place the tray on the circular table between the chairs.

'You said you weren't hungry, but I thought a glass of milk and sandwiches might be just what you needed,' he said, straightening and turning to face her. 'I hope you like ham and cheese.'

'That's . . . fine, thank you.' She stared at him, at his tawny hair brushed so severely back from his broad forehead, and the white shirt which seemed to be spanning too tightly across his wide shoulders. His eyes met hers, flicked down the length of her to her bare toes digging into the carpet, and up again to her face which had become flushed beneath his scrutiny. 'It was kind of you to go to all this trouble.' She managed to force the words past a throat which felt as if a restricting hand had gripped it.

'It was no trouble.' His voice was abrupt while his eyes probed and questioned. 'Are you still mad at me?'

'I was never mad at you, **Luke**,' she corrected hastily and ruefully. 'I was mad at myself, and I still am.'

'You pride yourself on always keeping a tight rein on your emotions, don't you, Amy.' It was a bold statement of fact, not a query. 'It's your pride that is hurt at the knowledge that you could have allowed yourself to enjoy something which ought to have been as natural as breathing.'

It felt as if he had struck her, and her face paled. It was true, her pride was hurt, but there was also a growing fear of something he would never understand.

They stared at each other in silence, her eyes filled with an inner anguish, his probing intently for an explanation she could not give him. The atmosphere was charged between them, and Amy's senses picked up the vibrations emanating from Luke. A weakness spilled into her limbs, and her heart was racing with a speed that quickened her breathing. If he touched her now she would be lost. She feared it, and yet she wanted it with a longing so intense that her body began to tremble in anticipation of those strong hands exploring her heated flesh.

The flicker of desire in Luke's eyes was unmistakable when his glance trailed over her slender body before returning to linger on her quivering lips. Amy had long since relinquished the effort to fight off a trembling expectancy, when Luke took a quick pace towards her but just as quickly turned away to rake his fingers through his hair.

'God, Amy, do you know what you're doing to me?' he demanded thickly, and disappointment mingled with relief as she continued to stare at him helplessly. 'No, I guess you don't,' he answered his own query harshly, 'and I'd better get out of here before I do or say something we might both regret.'

He strode out of her suite, and the lock clicked automatically into position when he closed the door behind him. The sound jarred her taut nerves, and she drew a quivering breath to discover that she was near to tears.

God, what is the matter with me? she wondered, collapsing into a chair when her legs gave way beneath her. What was it about Luke Tanner that he could take control of her mind and her body in this way and leave her almost without a will of her own? No man to date had ever succeeded in stripping her so completely of her composure, but Luke merely had to walk into the room to draw a reaction from her which was beginning to alarm her.

Amy pulled herself together with an effort. She was tired, and she was becoming over-emotional, she scolded herself. She ate the sandwiches and drank the milk Luke had brought her, and it was only when she had finished the lot that she realised how hungry she had actually been. Her hand rose to her mouth to stifle a yawn behind her fingers, and she stretched lazily. She *was* tired and, switching off the lights, she went to bed and slept soundly all night.

It was cloudy on Tuesday morning, but Amy was up early to check the film in her camera, and to make the necessary notes which she had been too tired to take care of the night before. The brochure advertising the tour was beginning to take shape in her mind, and if everything went as smoothly as it had up to now the first coastal tour ought to be on its way during the first week in November. That should please Luke, not to mention Uncle Ben, and since this was Amy's first big assignment since joining Aloe Tours, she was more determined than ever to make a success of it.

'I suggest we take a break in Durban and return to Cape Town on Saturday,' Luke announced when they drove away from Port St Johns that morning after breakfast. 'Do you think that it might inconvenience your uncle if you took a couple of days off from the office?'

'No, I don't imagine it would,' she admitted reluctantly. The thought of spending a few days in Durban with Luke did not appeal to her, but she supposed it would be unfair of her to expect him to attempt the long drive back immediately so she added, 'I think it might be advisable to spend a few days in Durban before driving back to Cape Town.'

'Good!' he said abruptly without taking his eyes off the road, and they lapsed into silence once again.

Luke was taking the scenic drive through Lusikisiki and Flagstaff to Kokstad, and they drove along forests and across rivers with unpronounceable names but always the countryside was lush and green. It was, in fact, quite breathtaking, and Amy was glad that she had thought to include this route in the tour she had mapped out.

It was after eleven that morning when they arrived at Margate, and it was lunchtime before Amy had all the information she required. They had a quick snack in the manager's office, and then they left on the last stretch of their journey to Durban.

The hotel on the Durban beachfront was a modern, magnificent, twenty-five-storeyed building with a wide, sweeping drive up to the pillared entrance. Their arrival was anticipated, as it had been at all the other hotels they had visited, and a uniformed black man appeared as if on call to take charge of Luke's Mercedes and their luggage while they entered the cool, air-conditioned building. A tall, blonde, elegantly clad woman disengaged herself from her discussion with the receptionist, and her attractive, delicately modelled features lit up with a welcoming smile as she approached them quickly across the thickly carpeted foyer.

'Luke!' the woman exclaimed softly, embracing him with a familiarity that made Amy feel a stab of envy she did not want to analyse. 'It's so good to see you again,' the woman added.

'Hello, my dear,' Luke smiled, brushing his lips against her cheek, and he kept an arm about her slender shoulders as he turned towards Amy. 'Janet, I'd like you to meet Amy Warren. Amy, this is Janet Hawkins. Janet's husband, Garth, manages this hotel, and Janet keeps an excellent set of books.'

Amy could not recall afterwards how she had responded to this introduction. She was conscious only of the way Luke was looking at Janet Hawkins, and she could scarcely believe that those rugged, sometimes harsh features could soften with such incredible warmth and tenderness.

'Where will I find Garth?' Luke's deep, baritone voice interrupted Amy's thoughts and her silent observation.

'The last time I saw him he was on his way to the conference room,' Janet Hawkins informed him with a warmth in her grey eyes which was beginning to make Amy wonder at something which was actually none of her business at all.

'I'll leave you in Janet's capable hands, Amy,' Luke announced, turning to face Amy again as if he had suddenly remembered that he and Janet were not alone. 'Janet will show you around, and she'll give you whatever information you need.'

Amy nodded coolly, and he walked away leaving her with this woman who was studying her now with speculative interest.

'Since Luke told us of this new venture I've been very anxious to meet you,' Janet enlightened Amy, and Amy did not quite know what to make of that remark. 'Shall we get down to business?'

Amy agreed, and for the next hour and a half she did not have time to think about anything but work. Janet Hawkins was a professional. She had all the information practically at her fingertips which made Amy's job so much easier, and she was not in the least put out at having to take Amy to the various places of interest in the hotel. Amy's camera clicked frequently as she took shots of the bathing area, the restaurants, the ornamental gardens, and the accommodation which visitors would have at their disposal. This was by far the most elaborate hotel in the Blue Dolphin group and Janet was obviously proud to play such an important role in the management.

'I don't think the men are going to join us for tea,' Janet remarked laughingly when they returned to her office. 'When Garth and Luke get together they usually have so much to talk about that they forget about everything else.'

Amy watched her pour tea into white cups with the blue dolphin emblem on the sides, and her curiosity could no longer be contained. 'Have you known each other a long time?'

'You could say we've known each other since the days we toddled about in nappies.' Janet laughed again, her friendly warmth reaching out to Amy as she continued to explain. 'We went to school together, we studied together at university, and we dreamed together of one day owning the best hotels in the country, but it didn't quite work out that way. It takes grit, determination, and nerves of steel to get where Luke is today, and Garth and I simply didn't measure up to those qualities. We opted out of the scheme when Luke took that initial gamble ten years ago. We felt the risk was simply too great, but Luke's gamble paid off, and that's why he is where he is today, while my husband and I are quite content to manage one of his hotels.'

'Don't you ever regret not going along with Luke's plans?'

'Oh, good heavens, no!' She looked surprised. 'We're extremely happy the way we are, and we've never doubted that we made the right decision.'

Amy did not linger after she had had her tea. Janet arranged with the porter to show her up to her suite on the twenty-fourth floor, and Amy did not relax entirely until she was alone in the set of rooms furnished in cool shades of blue. She walked towards the window overlooking the beachfront, but her mind was not on the magnificent view of the Indian Ocean. She was thinking about something Penny had said about Luke having been in love with the woman who had married his best friend. It had only been a rumour, her secretary had said, but Amy was beginning to wonder if there had not been some truth in it. She had seen the way he looked at Janet Hawkins, she had seen the tender affection in his smile, and the recollection made an odd tightness settle in her chest for which she could not find an explanation.

She met Garth Hawkins at dinner that evening.
He was a lean, dark-haired man who was not quite
as tall as Luke and whose attractive features were
less rugged. He was a very good-looking man, and
it was clear to Amy that he and his wife adored
each other. Amy found herself observing Luke
unobtrusively, but if Janet's love for her husband
affected him in any way, then he gave no sign of it.
They were, in fact, a very happy group together,
reminiscing at times about the past, but mostly
discussing future plans. Amy was not excluded
from their conversation, and when her opinion
was called for on certain matters they listened
attentively and grasped with interest at fresh ideas
to attract visitors to their hotel. Amy was glad,
too, that she did not have to spend the evening
alone with Luke, and when she eventually retired
to her suite she was relaxed and pleasantly tired.

Amy was awakened on the Wednesday morning
with the sun streaming into her bedroom, and she
stretched lazily before she got out of bed and
dressed herself in a cool cotton frock and sandals.
She ordered a light breakfast to be brought up to
her suite, and she ate it while she watched the
playground and beach filling up with holiday-
makers. It was going to be a warm, humid day, she
could feel it in the air, and she switched on the air-
conditioner before she sat down at the small desk
to read through the notes she had made on this
trip. She sorted them into order, and jotted down
a few improvements.

Knowing that she would not return to her office
before the following Monday, she took this
opportunity to start working in earnest on the
information for the brochure, and she was still
working on it an hour later when there was a
knock on her door.

'Come in, it's open!' she called, but a moment later a prickly sensation at the back of her neck made her swing round in her chair to see Luke entering and closing the door behind him.

Her heart skipped several beats at the sight of him, and she had to admit that he looked devastating in a white, towelling shirt, with navy slacks hugging his lean hips and muscular thighs, and white canvas shoes.

'I'd like you to come with me this morning.'

'Oh?' she murmured, confused and wary at the same time.

'Don't look so suspicious,' he smiled, his teeth white and strong against his tanned complexion. 'I'd like to take you along to someone whom I particularly want you to meet.'

'Someone in the hotel?' she asked cautiously.

'No,' he answered abruptly and without elaborating. 'Are you coming?'

Amy hesitated a moment, but decided at length that there was no harm in accepting his invitation. 'Give me a minute or so to clear away these papers and to run a comb through my hair.'

Luke nodded and lit a cigarette while Amy hastily gathered her papers together and put them away in her briefcase. She took her briefcase into the bedroom with her to lock it away, and she was running a comb through her hair when the telephone rang shrilly.

'Would you answer that, please?' she called from the bedroom, adding an extra touch of pale pink lipstick to her lips, and checking her appearance in the mirror.

'Tanner,' she heard Luke answering the telephone abruptly, and it was followed almost at once by a harsh exclamation that made her walk swiftly into the lounge. Luke's eyes, narrowed and icy, captured hers, and his mouth twisted derisively when he held out the receiver towards her. 'It's a Cape Town call for you ... *Mrs* Warren.'

The coldness that shifted over her heart could be attributed to two things. The first was the shattering coldness in Luke's eyes, and the second was the realisation that no one would call her from Cape Town unless there was something seriously wrong.

There was a slight tremor in her hand when she took the receiver from Luke and lifted it to her ear. 'Amy Warren speaking.'

'Amy!' her secretary's relieved voice crackled over the line. 'Gosh, am I glad I got hold of you!'

'What's the problem?' Amy asked abruptly, turning her back on Luke's glowering appraisal.

'Your uncle has picked up a virus, or something, and the doctor has booked him off for a week at least,' Penny informed her. 'Between Hilda and myself we'll manage to hold the fort for a while, but how soon do you think you could get back here?'

'I'll take the first available flight,' Amy promised, hoping that Luke would understand that this was an emergency.

'Oh, good!' Penny exclaimed, adding ruefully, 'sorry about this.'

'I'll be there as soon as I can,' Amy ended the conversation and, replacing the receiver on its cradle, she turned to face Luke who was now observing her with a stony expression on his face. 'Uncle Ben is ill,' she explained with a calmness she was far from experiencing, 'and I shall have to take the first available flight back to Cape Town.'

'I think you owe me an explanation, *Mrs* Warren.' There was no warmth in that deep voice, only a biting coldness that sliced into her marrow. 'You're not wearing a ring, so you've either got your husband tucked away somewhere out of sight, or you're divorced.'

'I'm *not* divorced and, in a manner of speaking, my husband *is* tucked away somewhere out of sight. I'm a widow,' she explained coldly, 'and it's really none of your business!'

The atmosphere was suddenly electrified as the whiteness of anger settled about his tight mouth. Why was he so angry? she wondered confusedly. Why was he behaving as if she had deliberately withheld something from him? She had not known him two weeks yet, and he was behaving as if she should have sat down and poured out her life history to him. *Who the hell did he think he was?* she asked herself with a sudden burst of inner anger.

'You're right, it is none of my business,' he said in a clipped, icy voice as he strode towards the door. 'Start packing while I make the necessary arrangements for your flight, and when you're ready I'll drive you to the airport.'

He had gone before she could say anything, and for some obscure reason she felt hot tears filling her eyes. She dashed them away angrily. She was being ridiculous, and for no reason at all.

Amy walked into the bedroom and hauled down her suitcase. She packed quickly, leaving out a linen skirt and jacket, and a neat blouse in which to travel. She was in the bathroom collecting her toiletries when reception telephoned to inform her that that she had been booked on to the eleven o'clock flight to Cape Town, and that Luke would be waiting for her in the foyer to depart for the airport at ten fifteen.

She glanced at her watch. She had a half-hour to

D

get herself ready and down to the foyer and, taking Luke's present mood into consideration, she had better not keep him waiting.

Luke was in the foyer to take Amy's suitcase from her when she stepped out of the lift, and he carried it out to his waiting car. His face was a tightly controlled mask that gave her no indication of what he was thinking, or feeling, and she could not image why it bothered her so much. They did not speak in the car on the way to Louis Botha airport, and the atmosphere was strained almost to breaking point.

'They'll have your ticket at the counter where you hand in your suitcase, and it's paid for,' Luke spoke to her for the first time when they entered the airport building.

'You didn't have to pay for it, Luke, but I'll refund——'

'Forget it!' he interrupted her harshly, handing over her suitcase when they reached the checkpoint. 'This is as far as I can go.'

'Please say goodbye to Janet and Garth for me, and thank them for their assistance and their hospitality.'

Luke nodded curtly.

'I'm sorry I've had to put you to so much trouble,' Amy added apologetically, and when Luke made no reply she realised that there was nothing else left to say. 'Goodbye, Luke,' she murmured, her throat tightening with those unexpected and inexplicable tears, and she turned away hastily to walk through the security entrance.

Her throat was still tight and aching with suppressed tears when the Boeing climbed steeply into the sky. *What is the matter with me?* she asked herself fiercely while she stared blindly out of the window beside her. Did it really matter that Luke was angry with her? No, it did not! She was simply tired, and she was confused, and . . . oh, what was the sense in trying to fool herself! She was treading on dangerous ground where Luke Tanner was concerned, and she would have to make an even greater effort to stay out of his way in future.

Amy arrived in Cape Town at two thirty that afternoon, and she took a taxi straight to the office where Penny and Hilda Lane, Uncle Ben's secretary, welcomed her with a cup of tea. She telephoned Aunt Dorothy for reassurance about her uncle's health, and only then did she settle down to the work which had piled up on her desk. Work was a marvellous antidote for emotional stress, and Amy plunged into it with a fierce determination.

CHAPTER SIX

BEN SMYTHE was indisposed for almost two weeks, and Amy was kept too busy to think about anything other than work. It was only when her uncle returned to the office that she realised she had not seen or heard from Luke during that time. She had not somehow expected that she would hear from him, but his silence did leave her considerably disturbed. The proofs for the brochure arrived from the printers, and Amy slipped them into an envelope which she addressed to Luke and sent along to Tanner House for his inspection and approval.

Two days passed without a word from Luke, but on the evening of the third day her doorbell rang at the flat, and she found Luke standing on her doorstep. He looked dark and dangerous in dark grey slacks and a black leather jacket, and Amy stared at him, her nerves leaping to attention while her heart beat out a message like a pagan drum.

'May I come in?' he asked in a clipped voice, and Amy stood aside, her mouth too dry to speak. He brushed past her to enter the lounge, and she immediately recognised the large brown envelope which he deposited unceremoniously on the low, cane table. 'I've returned the proofs, and I can't fault you on them,' he informed her when she closed the door and followed him into the lounge.

'Thanks,' she managed huskily, passing the tip of her tongue over her dry lips in an unconsciously provocative manner which made his tawny glance sharpen. 'You could have returned the proofs to the office with a messenger, you know.'

'I prefer personal contact to making use of a messenger service.' The rebuke in his voice was unmistakable as he took off his jacket, draped it across the back of a chair, and seated himself with his long legs stretched out in front of him. 'Would it have taken too much time and effort for you to bring them to my office personally?'

'No, but——' She gestured a little helplessly with her hands as she stood there looking down at him with her heart beating like a frightened bird in her throat at the sheer magnetism of this man. 'We didn't exactly part on the best of terms in Durban.'

'And do you blame me for the way I reacted?'

'Not entirely,' she had to admit, sinking down into the chair nearest to her when her legs started behaving as if they had suddenly become boneless, 'but you didn't have to behave as if I had committed an unforgivable indiscretion by not telling you that I had been married before. After all, Luke, we hardly know each other and, once the business side of our relationship has been dealt with, I doubt if we shall be seeing much of each other.'

'I wouldn't be too sure of that, if I were you,' he smiled derisively. 'I admit that I was knocked a bit off balance by the discovery that you've been married before, but I don't see that as a stumbling block.'

Should she ignore his remark, or ought she to feel threatened? Amy considered this for a moment before she chose to use the direct approach to stress her feelings on this matter. 'I believe I've told you before that I have no intention of getting emotionally, or physically involved with a man, and I meant it.'

'Any man?' he smiled in that twisted way of his.

'Or me in particular?'

'*Any* man,' she answered stiffly. 'And I believe I've also said that to you before.'

'Why, Amy?' His eyes were narrowed and intent upon her controlled features. 'And don't tell me to mind my own business.'

'It *isn't* really any of your business, is it?'

'No problem is insurmountable, Amy,' was his surprising reply. 'If you need help then I'm willing to give it, but I can't do that if you don't trust me.'

Just what did he think her problem was? she wondered, hovering precariously between laughter and tears. 'Why—why would you want to help me?'

'Oh, I don't know,' he smiled lazily, his glance flicking over her pink and white, candy-striped dress which buttoned up all the way down the front, and she had a suffocating notion that he was mentally undoing each big, pearly button. 'Perhaps it's because I happen to like brown eyes flecked with gold, or maybe it's because I have a desire to see you laugh more often the way you laughed that night on the beach when we got ourselves soaked.'

She thought at first that he was mocking her, but his expression had altered while he spoke, and there was something in the way he was looking at her now that made her realise that he was absolutely serious. A lump rose in her throat, and she swallowed it with difficulty. 'Stop being so nice to me, Luke.'

She had risen to her feet agitatedly, but Luke had also risen, and his hands gripped her shoulders with a firmness that made her suspect he could snap her fragile bones if he so wished.

'Would you rather I bashed you about?' he demanded as if he was quite prepared to do exactly that.

'No, of course not!' she shook her head, keeping her eyes on a level with a button half-way down the front of his open-necked shirt.

'Then what do you want?' He shook her slightly.

'Oh, Luke!' His name tripped off her lips in something between a plea and a laugh. 'Why do you insist on making life difficult for me?'

'I could ask you that same question,' he countered harshly, releasing her abruptly to comb his fingers agitatedly through his hair which never failed to remind her of a lion's mane. 'God, Amy, I can't tell you how many hours I've spent trying to unravel the mystery surrounding you.'

She felt herself tense. 'There is no mystery. I simply don't want to— —'

'Get involved with any man and, I'm beginning to think, least of all with me!' he interrupted her almost savagely as he swung round to pin her down with a blazing glance. 'Don't tell me you're determined to remain loyal to the memory of a man who's dead, because I just won't accept that!'

'I have enough sense to know one can't remain loyal to a memory!' she retorted icily. 'Now, may we *please* change the subject?'

There had been tension between them before, but at that moment the atmosphere was positively crackling. She wanted him to go and leave her alone, and she guessed that he knew it, but the unrelenting set of his jaw warned her that he was not going to grant her her wish.

'Are you going to offer me a cup of coffee, or would that be stretching your hospitality too far?'

Amy had never been so torn between anger and laughter, but she gave in to neither as she raised her chin defiantly to meet his tawny glance. 'Never let it be said that I was inhospitable.'

She turned on her heel and, aware of his eyes boring into her back, she marched into the kitchen. She switched on the electric kettle, set out two cups, and spooned instant coffee into them, but she was not thinking about what she was doing. It was Luke's biting remark that continued to echo through her mind. *Don't tell me you're determined to remain loyal to the memory of a man who's dead.* That was ridiculous! If anything, Luke had shown her exactly how totally *dis*loyal she could be to Keith's memory.

Amy almost spilled boiling water over her hand and the cupboard top when she heard music coming from the lounge. It was the instrumental version of an old song, 'As Time Goes By', but she knew the words by heart.

Did he deliberately choose that record to remind her of the first and only time he had kissed her? Her heart was beating heavily in her breast, and her hands were trembling when she carried the tray of coffee through to the lounge to find Luke sprawled in his chair with his eyes closed so that she noticed for the first time the extraordinary length and thickness of his dark lashes. He opened his eyes at once, as if he had sensed her presence, and he smiled apologetically.

'I hope you don't mind?' he said, shifting his large frame into an upright position on the chair. 'I was looking through your records, and that particular song happens to be a favourite of mine.'

Amy felt a stab of incredulity, and she hoped he did not notice the tremor in her hand when she handed him his cup of coffee. 'It's a favourite of mine too.'

'It reminds me of the conversation we had on the beach that night in Port Elizabeth,' he said thoughtfully while he stirred his coffee. 'We must take time off from the strenuous lives we lead to remember that the fundamental things in life still apply, despite all the technological and scientific advances we've made.'

Yes, the fundamental things did still apply, but she could do without the kissing, the sighing, and the loving. It hurt too much.

The song ended, and the hi-fi needle shifted on to the next track on the record while they drank their coffee and talked. Amy felt her nerves unravelling slowly, and an hour later when Luke got up to leave, she was almost sorry to see him go.

'Thank you, Amy.'

His hand rested heavily on her shoulder, its warmth burning her through the cotton of her frock as she looked a long way up into his tawny eyes. 'Why are you thinking me?'

'For helping me to relax and unwind.' His hand slid beneath her hair, and the touch of his fingers against the nape of her neck aroused sensations which were almost electrifying. 'Good night, Amy.'

He lowered his head, brushing his lips against hers in a feather-light kiss, and then he was gone, leaving her standing there with a bemused look on her face.

Luke Tanner was the most extraordinary man she had ever met. His brilliant mind had placed him in a position in society where he was often feared and revered, he could count among his friends several high-ranking officials in the country, and he could afford to indulge himself in almost any way he pleased. He had mentioned a skiing holiday in Switzerland which would remain merely a dream for most people, and yet he could enjoy the simple pleasure of wading barefoot through the shallow waters on a beach. He was a complex man, a man with a masculine appeal which would leave no woman untouched, and yet Amy could relax with him and talk to him in a way she had not been able to talk to any man before . . . not even Keith, whom she had known almost all her life.

'Take care, Amy!' she warned herself. 'You're walking into something with your eyes wide open, and that could take you exactly where you don't want to go!'

She lay awake in bed that night. She was sleepy, but her mind would not let her rest. Despite all her efforts to the contrary, she liked Luke, and she admired and respected him for what he was. His aversion to the commitment of marriage did not trouble her at all. It was his business entirely if he wanted to be free to flit from one woman to the next, but she had no intention of having her name added to his long list of conquests. She would not see him again when the business side of their relationship came to an end, and that would be that.

Amy turned over on to her side and snuggled down beneath the covers. Now that she had sorted everything out in her mind she ought to go to sleep, but sleep evaded her for some time while she fought against the odd sensation that she might succeed in banishing Luke Tanner from her life, but never quite from her mind.

During the ensuing week Amy spoke to Luke several times on the telephone, but their conversations had been brief and impersonal. The only time she had seen him was at the attorney's office for the signing of the contract, and this meeting had been equally brief. He had rushed off to another appointment immediately after attaching his bold signature to the documents, and Amy had returned to her office with Uncle Ben in a faintly bewildered frame of mind. She did not want to get involved with Luke, and yet his aloof manner touched her on the raw for some obscure reason.

The intercom buzzed on her desk on Friday morning, two days after the signing of the contract, and she put down her pen to flick the appropriate switch.

'Mr Tanner on line one for you, Amy,' her secretary informed her.

'Thank you, Penny.' Amy's hand trembled as she flicked the switch back into its original position, pressed the button for line one, and lifted the telephone receiver.

'Hello, Luke,' she answered, her voice schooled for yet another brief business discussion.

'What are you doing this evening, Amy?'

His query startled her to such an extent that for a moment she could not think straight. 'I . . . well, nothing in particular. Why do you ask?'

'I'd like you to come and have dinner with me at my home.'

Did he think she was an idiot to fall for an invitation such as this? 'It's kind of you to invite me, but I don't think——'

'We shan't be alone, if that's what you're thinking,' he interrupted her with that increasingly familiar hint of mockery in his voice that sent a rush of blood into her face.

'In that case I accept,' she answered coolly, taking it for granted that this would be a business dinner of sorts.

'Be ready at seven,' he instructed. 'I'll send my car to collect you at your flat.'

The line went dead before she could protest, and

she sat there staring at the instrument in her hand as if she could not recall how it had got there.

She slammed the receiver back on to its cradle and cursed silently. Luke Tanner somehow had the ability to rattle her composure and leave her feeling like an adolescent. He would speak to her one minute with that abrupt note of authority in his deep voice, and the next he would mock her. She never quite knew whether she was on her head or her heels, and when she was thoroughly confused, he would turn on that devastating charm to make her feel weak at the knees. The man was most infuriating!

Amy fumed her way through the rest of that morning. The afternoon was no better, but when she went home that evening she found that she was preparing herself with a great deal more care than usual.

Her skin was silky smooth and scented after her bath, and her black hair had been brushed until it hung in heavy, glossy waves over her slim shoulders. Her dress was the colour of deep red wine, and the full skirt flared out from the gathered waistline. The sleeveless bodice was loose-fitting, and gathered on the shoulders in a faintly Grecian design. It complemented her colouring, and it gave her a Latin look which she could not claim in her ancestry.

Amy was applying a light touch of her favourite perfume when her doorbell rang promptly at seven and, snatching up her wrap and her handbag, she walked quickly out of her room.

Standing on her doorstep was an elderly black man in a grey suit and peaked cap, and he smiled, raising his cap politely. 'Mr Tanner sent me to fetch you,' he explained.

Amy nodded and smiled back into that friendly

face as she locked her door and accompanied him out of the building to the silver-grey Mercedes parked in the street. The rear door was opened for her, and Amy got in, gathering the folds of her dress about her before he closed the door and walked round to the driver's side to get in behind the wheel.

The drive into the city and out to Bishops Court took less time than she had imagined it would. The lights of the Mercedes pierced the darkness as the road twisted and turned among the trees, and then they were slowing down to pass beneath the concrete-pillared arch.

The paved driveway dipped down at once, circling a house that looked like a fortress in the darkness with its turrets etched against the night sky. It was surrounded by trees, some of them indigenous, and their branches swayed in the wind which had blown up across Table Bay. The driver brought the Mercedes to a halt directly below the stone steps leading up to the entrance, and there was a tightening at the pit of her stomach when she glanced up at the house which seemed to tower frighteningly above her. Lights, like two full moons, were perched on the pillars at the base of the steps, and Amy was half-way up the half-dozen steps when Luke appeared above her on the well-lit patio. He looked as menacing as his fortress in black slacks and black shirt, and her heart skipped a frightened beat.

'Thank you, William,' he addressed the elderly black man, then he held out his hand to Amy. 'Come in out of this wind.'

Her hand disappeared into his, his touch sending a shaft of feeling through her that left her nerves quivering, and she was ushered into the impressive stone fortress which was his home.

The interior was not as she had imagined it would be. The entrance hall was spacious with a winding staircase leading to the upper floor. The furnishings were modern, and strategically placed spotlights illuminated a large ewer in Venetian glass, a potted palm, and an original Paul Cézanne still life which must have cost a fortune to acquire.

She was led into the living-room, her gold, high-heeled sandals sinking into the thick pile of the carpet, and here too the décor was modern. The colour was predominantly white, with a touch of green in the curtains and carpet to break the starkness.

Luke thrust his hands into his pockets and studied her through narrowed eyes. 'Do you like it?'

'Very much,' she admitted, casting an expectant glance about the room and finding it empty except for Luke and herself. 'Am I the first to arrive?'

'You're the only guest,' he smiled lazily, his glance flicking over her with a glitter of something more than appreciation in his eyes, and her anger rose like a surging tide inside her.

'You lied to me!' she accused, her dark eyes blazing up into his. 'You said we wouldn't be alone, and ... oh, how *could* you, Luke?'

His hands gripped her shoulders and he spun her round so that she was facing the door. A woman with silvery hair was entering the living-room, and eyes the colour of Luke's studied Amy with a hint of curiosity in their depths.

'Amy, I'd like you to meet my mother,' Luke said behind her. 'Mother, this is Amy Warren.'

Amy stared at the woman in the cinnamon-coloured dress who was walking towards them, and she felt curiously as if someone had winded her.

'My dear, I'm so happy to meet you at last,' Mrs Tanner smiled, both hands outstretched to take Amy's. 'Luke has told me so much about you, and I was looking forward to our meeting in Durban, but unfortunately you had to leave in rather a hurry, I believe.'

So, it was his mother Luke had wanted her to meet that Wednesday morning, before the call had come through from Penny to tell her about her uncle. How strange, Amy thought while she murmured the appropriate words of greeting. Did he take all his lady friends to meet his mother?

'What would you like to drink before dinner, Amy?' Luke interrupted the trend of her confused thoughts.

'A glass of wine, thank you,' she answered him while she fought to regain her composure.

'White or red?'

'White, please.'

'What about you, Mother?' Luke enquired of the woman who had seated herself gracefully on the padded sofa beside a white porcelain table lamp with a leaf-green shade.

'I'll have a glass of white wine as well, thank you,' his mother smiled up at him, then her glance returned to Amy, and she patted the seat beside her with a hand on which diamonds glittered. 'Come and sit here next to me, Amy, and tell me what my big, bad son has been up to that you were so angry with him when I walked in.'

'I actually owe Luke an apology, Mrs Tanner,' Amy smiled ruefully, seating herself beside the older woman and letting her glance follow Luke's broad-shouldered frame as he walked towards the glass cabinet beneath a watercolour landscape of Table Mountain. 'When he invited me to have dinner here this evening he said that we wouldn't be alone, but, when I arrived and found that I was the only guest, I accused him of lying to me.'

Luke turned his head, his mocking glance colliding with hers. 'Your apology is accepted, Amy.'

'And I'm very glad to meet a young woman who still makes an effort to live up to certain standards and the moral codes of the old society,' his mother announced, smiling at Amy, but her expression became censorious when she glanced at Luke who was approaching them with a long-stemmed glass of wine in each hand. 'If you harm this girl in any way, Luke, you shall have me to answer to.'

'My dear Mother, I have never harmed a woman in my life, and I have no intention of doing so now.' His eyebrows had risen in sardonic amusement as he handed them their drinks. 'Whose side are you on, anyway?'

Amy sat rigidly on the edge of her seat, not sure whether she ought to feel flattered or embarrassed by the trend of their conversation.

'It's not a matter of taking sides, Luke,' his mother answered him with a spark of humour emerging from the gravity in her voice. 'I haven't exactly approved of the life you have led up to now, but I'm happy to see that you have at last met a woman who is not going to let you have everything your own way.'

'You're right there, Mother,' he laughed shortly, his tawny eyes meeting Amy's as he lowered himself into a chair and swallowed a mouthful of whisky from the goblet he nursed in his hand. 'I'm beginning to despair that Amy will ever let me have my way with her,' he added with a wicked gleam in his eyes.

'Luke!' the older woman gasped, an outraged expression on her face while Amy wished she could sink into the cushions beneath her, and hide there.

'Forgive me, Amy,' he said at once, 'but I couldn't resist that remark, and you're beautiful when you blush.'

Amy swallowed down a mouthful of wine to hide her confusion, and moments later a white-coated coloured man announced that dinner would be served.

The walls in the dining-room had been painted an antique coral, the woodwork was white, and various articles in blue and white china were displayed on shelves which had been built into the north-facing wall. The dresser and chairs were of yellowwood and stinkwood, and a white, damask tablecloth covered the long oval table on which the silverware gleamed beneath the crystal chandelier that hung from the ceiling.

They were seated far apart, with Luke at the head of the table, his mother on his right, and Amy on his left. It looked rigidly formal, but Luke and his mother made it delightfully informal with their bantering conversation which was laced heavily with the fondness they felt for each other.

Tomato soup was served in delicate china bowls, and it was followed by roast lamb, tiny potatoes, and an assortment of vegetables which had been prepared and served with a mouthwatering excellence.

'Luke has been telling me about the new coastal tour between Cape Town and Durban,' Mrs Tanner steered the conversation towards a topic which was very much on Amy's mind. 'When do you expect the first coach tour to leave from Cape Town?'

'The date is set for the first Monday of November,' Amy informed her, making a swift mental calculation. 'That's in three weeks' time.'

Luke's mother was eager to know all the details,

and Amy dutifully listed all the places of interest which would be visited by the tourists. Luke did not contribute to this conversation, he merely sat there at the head of the table with a look of amusement flashing periodically across his rugged face when Amy had to relinquish an attempt to eat in order to answer yet another query of his mother's. Amy did not mind, she found it exciting to talk about the tour and the way their plans were progressing. Mrs Tanner was also a very attentive audience and, if Amy had been nervous earlier that evening, she now found herself relaxing completely during a meal which lasted more than an hour.

'You have been very quiet throughout dinner, Luke,' his mother accused when they had returned to the living-room and were drinking their coffee.

'That's not surprising, Mother,' Luke answered in a lazy drawl. 'You have been monopolising the attention of my guest, and I'm jealous.'

His mother's eyes widened in consternation. 'Oh dear, have I really?'

'No, Mrs Tanner. Luke is teasing, I'm sure, and I've enjoyed talking to you very much.' Amy placed a reassuring hand on the older woman's arm, glared briefly at Luke, and changed the subject. 'How long are you staying?'

'I'm booked back on the Monday morning flight to Durban.'

'So soon?' Amy asked, having discovered during dinner that Luke's mother had arrived only two days ago.

'Luke will also be leaving on Monday,' Mrs Tanner enlightened Amy, her glance swerving towards her son who sat sprawled in his chair with his long legs stretched out in front of him. 'You'll be staying in Johannesburg for a week or more, won't you, dear?' she sought confirmation from him.

'That's correct,' Luke smiled, his glance colliding once again with Amy's, and her heart fluttered like a bird trapped in a gentle, but confining hand.

'Why don't you come and have lunch with us on Sunday?' Mrs Tanner asked, and Amy dragged her startled glance from Luke's to look at the woman seated close to her on the sofa.

'Oh, I—I don't know, I——' Amy halted her stammering reply to regain her scattered wits. 'It will be your last day here with Luke, and I would simply be in the way.'

'Nonsense, my dear, we would love to have you join us,' the older woman brushed aside Amy's tentative refusal. 'Isn't that so, Luke?'

'You're quite right, Mother,' Luke agreed smoothly, that lazy smile in his tawny eyes capturing Amy's glance and holding it with frightening ease. 'Say *yes*, sweet Amy?' he invited, his deep voice warm and persuasive.

Amy felt driven into a corner. Her instincts warned her to refuse, but, if she did so, his mother might wonder at the reason, and Amy was not in a position to explain.

'Thank you, I—I'd love to come,' she heard herself saying, and there was a flicker of triumph in Luke's eyes that made her hate him at that moment.

'Good, that's settled, then!' Mrs Tanner exclaimed delightedly, unaware of the tension which had risen between her son and Amy.

Mrs Tanner's delightful conversation kept Amy there for yet another hour, and it was after ten o'clock when she thanked them for the superb dinner and announced that it was time she left.

'I'll take you home,' said Luke, getting to his feet. 'I'll bring the car round to the entrance.'

He walked out of the house, leaving Amy to gather up her wrap and her handbag, and his mother graciously accompanied Amy into the hall. The sound of the Ferrari pulling up in front of the house ended their conversation, and Amy said a hasty good night to the silvery-haired woman before leaving the house the way she had entered it earlier.

The wind had subsided slightly, but it was still strong enough to tug at her skirt and whip her hair about her face. Luke leaned over to open the door on the passenger side for her, and she got in quickly. The powerful thrust of the Ferrari's engine forced her back against her seat as it sped up the drive towards the pillared entrance, and her fingers tightened about her bag. She had always disliked speed, and she hoped that Luke was not planning to give her an impromptu demonstration of the Ferrari's capabilities.

Amy had been unnecessarily concerned. Luke was not a maniac behind the wheel of his red Ferrari. He drove fast, but she had the comforting feeling that he was in complete control at all times.

'You're very quiet, Amy,' he broke the silence between them when he had turned on to the N1 towards Bellville. 'Did my mother tire you out?'

'Oh, no!' she exclaimed almost indignantly. 'I think your mother is a warm-hearted, intelligent woman, and I enjoyed talking to her.'

'Why are you so quiet, then?'

'I was wondering . . .' She paused for reflection. She had been wondering about so many things, but one matter had taken priority. 'Why doesn't your mother live with you?'

'I have tried many times to persuade her to stay,' Luke explained, 'but my mother is Durban born and bred, and she prefers the climate up there.'

'I take it you are also originally from Durban?'

'I was born there, I grew up there, and I studied there at the university, but I've been living all over the place since I completed my studies.' He glanced at her briefly, the amber-coloured street lights adding a touch of fire to his eyes. 'Where were you born, Amy?'

Questioning Luke about himself had been easy, but it was a little more difficult having to answer questions about herself.

'I was born in Johannesburg,' she answered him reluctantly. 'I lived there all my life until . . .'

'Until your husband died?' he filled in for her when her voice faded into silence.

'Yes.'

'What made you break away and come to Cape Town?'

She did not want to think about that particular time in her life. The trauma of it had nearly killed her, but she had to give Luke a truthful answer. 'I had no—no family other than Uncle Ben, and when he—he suggested a complete change I—I thought it a good idea.'

'And that was four years ago?'

'Yes.'

Four years ago. Four long years of self-imposed exile. Amy felt her insides jolt at her own thoughts. *Self-imposed exile?* Why should she see it that way now?

CHAPTER SEVEN

THE silence between Amy and Luke had not been strained during the remainder of the drive to Bellville, although a certain amount of confusion was reigning in Amy's mind when they arrived at her flat. She was inexplicably unsure of herself, like someone groping for support in an attempt to balance herself after missing a step, and she could not understand the reason for it.

Luke took her keys from her to unlock the door to her flat, but alarm spiralled through her when he followed her inside and closed the door behind him.

'Thank you for a lovely evening, Luke,' she said hastily, hoping he would take the hint and go.

'It was my pleasure,' he smiled wryly as if he had read her thoughts. 'We shall expect you at about eleven on Sunday, and bring your swimsuit along if it's a nice day.'

'It's still too cold to swim,' she protested, thinking that he had to be joking.

'Not if the pool is heated.'

Amy considered this disclosure for a moment, then she smiled faintly. 'You're very fortunate.'

'I think I'm only just beginning to realise how fortunate I actually am.' She could not even begin to imagine what he meant by that, but his glance was lingering on her lips, and it told her something that made her alarm spiral higher. She turned away abruptly, intending to put a safer distance between them, but his hands gripped her shoulders with a bruising firmness, and she was spun round

to face him. 'Look at me, Amy,' he instructed
when she stubbornly kept her eyes lowered.

'It's late, Luke, and I've had a tiring day,' she
protested.

'Look at me!' He did not need to raise his voice
for her to realise he had issued a command, not a
request, and she was forced to obey. She raised her
eyes to his, and her pulse rate quickened at the
leaping fires in his tawny gaze. 'I shan't keep you
much longer,' he said, 'but there is something I've
been wanting to do all evening, and you're not
going to deny me that little pleasure.'

She knew what was going to happen, but she
was powerless to prevent it. His hard arms crushed
her against him, moulding her body to his in a way
that left her in no doubt as to what he actually
wanted. She turned her head away to avoid his
descending mouth, but he grasped a fistful of her
silky hair, applying a pressure on her scalp that
forced her face out into the open. Her lips parted
in a belated attempted to cry out in protest, but his
mouth descended at that moment to capture the
sweet moisture of hers with an expertise that made
her senses reel.

Luke had kissed her before, and she had been
prepared for that well of emotional turmoil she
would be plunged into, but this time an aching,
quivering warmth erupted inside her that awakened
a need so intense that she was clinging weakly to
his shoulders when he finally eased his mouth
from hers.

'Good night, Amy,' he smiled down into her
dazed and bewildered eyes. 'See you Sunday at
eleven.'

Amy stood leaning against the wall for support
for several seconds after Luke had left, and there
was a stunned look on her face. She had been

incapable of speech after he had kissed her, and she was still incapable of thinking one coherent thought. She pushed herself away from the wall to go to her bedroom and tripped over her handbag and her wrap which had fallen to the floor at some time during that soul-shattering kiss. She bent down to pick them up and walked on into her bedroom in a trance-like state, and it was only when she caught sight of herself in the full-length mirror that she came slowly to her senses. Her hair was dishevelled, her eyes were so bright they were almost feverish, and her cheeks were flushed a deep pink. Her lips seemed fuller, softer, and they were still throbbing and tingling with the memory of that masculine mouth which had taken possession of them.

'God, Amy, you must be going mad!' she addressed her image in the mirror in a voice that was too husky to be her own. 'What do you think you're doing to let that man get under your skin the way you have?'

She spun away angrily from her reflected image, and went through her usual ritual of undressing and creaming off her make-up. Her hands would not stop shaking, and she almost spilled cleansing liquid on to her dressing-table. This was ridiculous! Luke had kissed her, and her foundations were suddenly shuddering beneath her. She got into bed and switched off the light, her body lying rigid between the sheets. Her mind was beginning to function like a wheel grinding slowly into motion. So many things had been locked away securely inside her, but suddenly it all spilled out into her conscious mind with a clarity that made her sit up in bed as if she had been jolted by several volts of electricity.

She was in love with Luke!

The muscles in her body relaxed like the taut strings of a violin snapping one after the other until she sagged back limply against the pillows. She knew now why she had been afraid of him from the start, and she knew also why his aloof and abrupt manner during this past week had affected her in such an odd way. *She did not want to love him!* Falling in love had no place in the life she had mapped out for herself, but suddenly it was there, like the steel door of a cage slamming shut, and she was trapped. Her mind rejected it fiercely, she could already feel that dreaded pain of loving a man who would turn from her the moment somone else caught his fancy, and now there were no barriers behind which she could hide from her agony.

Pain was a strange thing at that moment. It opened doors she herself had locked four years ago, and it made her see herself for what she really was. She had been a coward. She had barricaded herself into a cocoon where her personal safety had been her only concern, and she had allowed the reality of life to pass her by because she had not had the stamina to face it. She could do something about the knowledge that she had been a coward, but how was she going to cope with that ever-present fear of being hurt again?

She wrestled with this problem for long hours without finding a solution, and it was almost dawn when she finally drifted into an exhausted sleep from which she did not awaken until noon the next day.

Amy had still not succeeded in solving her problem on Sunday morning when she left her flat and drove out to Bishops Court. She was wary of coming face to face with Luke now that she knew how she felt about him. She had no idea how she would react, and she was desperately afraid that she might do something to make him suspect that she cared. It was of some consolation knowing that Luke's mother would be there, and she clung to that thought as she neared his home on that warm October morning.

Luke's home did not look like a fortress at all in the daylight. The walls were of stone, the turrets were still there, but it was an attractive mixture of medieval and modern architecture which was pleasing rather than frightening to the eye.

Amy was nervous when she walked up the stone steps to the front door and rang the bell. Mrs Tanner opened the door, and a smile creased her lined but attractive face as her glance took in Amy's slim figure in the summer frock which was a floral mixture of blue, green and gold.

'Come in, my dear,' she invited graciously. 'Luke is taking a business call in the study, but he'll join us in a moment.'

'It's a gorgeous day, isn't it?' Amy remarked simply for the sake of saying something as she stepped into the hall. She was trying to hide the fact that she was nervous, but she knew somehow that she was not succeeding when Mrs Tanner darted a quick, curious glance at her.

'Lovely,' the older woman agreed somewhat absently, linking her arm through Amy's as she led her across the hall and down a few steps into a sunroom where the colour of the furnishings was a bright golden-yellow on a snow-white background. Potted plants added a touch of green to a room which was obviously frequently used, judging by the presence of a hi-fi and television set built into the wall. 'I've planned a cold lunch out on the patio near the pool,' Mrs

Tanner explained, 'and I'm so glad the weather has not disappointed me.'

She slid open the glass doors leading out on to the shaded patio, and beyond this was a sizeable pool with its crystal-clear water shimmering in the sunlight. The entire area was surrounded by a high wall with creepers trailing along it, and comfortable sun loungers with colourful umbrellas added to the peace and tranquillity emanating from this part of the house. Doves called to each other in the trees beyond the wall, and Amy felt as if she had stepped into a little part of Eden.

She sighed and exclaimed spontaneously, 'What a marvellous place to relax in!'

'That's exactly what I intended it to be,' Luke's deep baritone voice remarked directly behind her, and her breath locked in her throat as she spun round to face him. Tawny eyes smiled down into hers, then dipped lower to settle on that telltale pulse beating erratically at the base of her throat. 'Hello, Amy.'

Amy stared up at him as if she was seeing him for the first time in her life. She tried to speak, but her tongue seemed to cling stubbornly to the roof of her mouth. Oh, God, don't let me make a complete idiot of myself! she prayed silently, her glance locked with his as if she had been hypnotised by the strange lights flickering in his eyes.

'Would you like something cool to drink, Amy?' Mrs Tanner saved the situation. 'An iced fruit juice, perhaps?'

Amy somehow gathered her scattered wits about her and, dragging her glance almost forcibly from Luke's, she turned to the woman who had addressed her. 'That would be lovely, thank you.'

'Sit down, Mother, and I'll pour,' Luke instructed.

'Come, Amy,' Mrs Tanner smiled, indicating several chairs grouped around a slatted wooden table. 'Let's sit here in the shade.'

Amy sat down and did her best to concentrate on what Mrs Tanner was saying, but her glance was irresistibly drawn towards Luke. His sleeveless white T-shirt accentuated the width of his shoulders and displayed his tanned, muscled arms to perfection. Dark blue shorts hugged his lean hips, and left his long, muscular legs exposed down to the blue canvas shoes on his feet. His physique was magnificent, and Amy could barely drag her eyes away from him when he turned and walked towards them with their fruit drinks.

'Your drink, Mother,' he interrupted the practically one-side conversation, and Mrs Tanner looked up at him and smiled as she accepted her drink from him.

'Thank you, Luke.'

'Amy?' Their eyes met as she took the glass from him, and her hand was suddenly shaking to such an extent that he had to place his free hand over hers to steady the glass. 'Careful,' he warned softly.

'Thank you,' she murmured, her colour deepening, and her heart racing at his touch.

Dammit! She was behaving like an adolescent who was falling in love for the first time in her life, and that . . . that wasn't so! *Was it?*

Amy paled as she found herself confronted by yet another truth. She had loved Keith, but she had never loved him as a woman should love the man she had married. They had simply grown together over the years until they had believed that the only thing left for them was marriage. There had been no spark to ignite a fire between them; only a warm, comfortable glow, and a mutual fondness and understanding which had kept their life together on an even keel.

She looked up, directly into Luke's narrowed eyes, and her heart lurched violently in her breast. His piercing, probing glance in the wake of this new discovery was something she could not afford to prolong, and she lowered her eyes hastily to the glass of fruit juice in her hands which she had barely touched.

'I'm not looking forward to my flight to Durban tomorrow,' Mrs Tanner sighed, her expression conveying that she would have preferred to spend more time with her son.

'I'm not looking forward to the week I have to spend in Johannesburg,' Luke responded.

'I could always cancel.' Mrs Tanner studied her son hopefully, and with some amusement. 'What about you, Luke?'

'I'm afraid I can't cancel, but I'd give anything at this moment if I could.' He was looking at Amy while he spoke, making it obvious that he would have preferred to stay with her, and she once again felt that embarrassing warmth sliding into her cheek. 'Will you miss me, Amy?'

Amy paused for consideration, giving herself this opportunity to regain her composure before she said, 'I shall be too busy to give you a thought.'

Luke's laughter was a low rumble which seemed to originate from deep within his chest, and Amy liked the sound of it.

'She certainly has the ability to dent a man's ego, hasn't she, Mother?'

'It's a very good thing she knows how to put you in your place, and I hope she keeps you there,' was the only sympathy he received, and he grimaced.

'I have the distinct feeling that I'm on the losing side today.'

His mother laughed at his pained expression, and so did Amy. The tension seemed to ease out of the atmosphere, or perhaps it was simply that Amy had rid herself of the tension which had gripped her since early that morning.

Mrs Tanner excused herself eventually and, leaving Amy alone with Luke for the first time that morning, she went into the house to check on the lunch.

'Did you bring your swimsuit with you?' Luke broke the silence between them before it could become strained.

'I have it here,' she gestured to the canvas bag she had placed beside her chair.

'Let's a have swim before lunch,' he suggested, rising to his feet. 'I'll show you to the guest room where you can change.'

His arm brushed against hers when they entered the house, and the current of awareness that shot through her made her want to run like a frightened hare, but she controlled herself and put a safer distance between them as they crossed the hall and walked up that winding, carpeted staircase. He turned to the left when they reached the upper floor, and he opened the first door on his right.

'I'll meet you down at the pool,' he said, and she felt his eyes on her as he stood aside for her to enter, but he did not linger and continued down the passage in long, firm strides.

She stepped farther into the room and closed the door behind her. It was an attractive room, and the double bed had an antique French brass bedstead which added a touch of romance to it. The duvet and the curtains were a pale apricot, and oriental rugs lay scattered across the polished,

wooden floor. She placed her bag on the stool in
front of the antique dressing-table, and zipped it
open to take out her one-piece swimsuit and short
towelling robe. She changed quickly and exchanged
her high-heeled sandals for low, soft-soled shoes
with colourful canvas straps over the bridge of the
foot and, with her beach towel draped over her
arm, she left the room.

Amy felt awkward walking through the house in
her beach robe which reached only half-way down
to her knees, but she was being silly, and she knew
it. If only she did not feel so terribly vulnerable!

Luke was in the pool when she walked through the
sunroom and out on to the patio, and her nerves
quivered at the pit of her stomach when he turned
over on to his back in the water and saw her.

'Come on in, Amy,' he instructed, sliding his
hands over his wet hair. 'You'll find the water
refreshing.'

She dropped her towel on to a sun lounger
beside the pool, and took off her robe to expose
the emerald-green swimsuit which clung to her
slender body like a second skin. There was no need
for embarrassment, she had a good figure, but
Luke was watching her, and he always succeeded
in making her aware of her body in a way no other
man had ever done before. She could not look at
him when she walked towards the shallow steps
leading into the pool, but she felt his eyes on her,
roaming over her soft, feminine curves, and it was
a disturbing sensation.

The water was delightfully cool, not icy against
her heated flesh, and she swam slowly towards the
opposite side of the pool. She was aware of Luke
following her, but her enjoyment overshadowed
her nervousness, and she turned over on to her
back to float lazily on the water.

'Hm ... this is lovely,' she murmured when he reached her side and stopped to tread water.

'Lovely,' Luke agreed, his smile sensuous as his eyes roamed over her.

'Race you to the other side,' she challenged in an attempt to overcome her embarrassment.

Amy had speed in the water, but Luke's powerful strokes were more than a match for her, and he reached the opposite side seconds before her. Her heart was pounding when she clung to the tiled edge, and she was gasping for breath. 'I'm out of practice,' she laughed the moment she got her breath back.

'You're a strong swimmer,' he acknowledged, his eyes probing her body beneath the water, 'and that's quite something for someone so small and fragile.'

'I may be small, but I'm not fragile,' she declared indignantly, flicking her wet hair away from her face.

'I shan't argue with you, but when I look at you sometimes I get the feeling you're made of delicate porcelain.' His eyes seemed to darken when his glance lingered on the thin, stretchy material clinging to her rounded breasts and hardened nipples. 'You're beautiful, Amy.'

The tempo of her heartbeat altered to a nervous flutter. 'I think I've had enough swimming for one day.'

'I think you're running away from me,' he accused mockingly, but he did not stop her when she swam towards the steps and climbed out.

He followed her out of the pool, the water dripping from his body, and the dark hair on his limbs and chest clinging to his wet, sun-browned skin. His red swimming trunks were moulded to his lean hips, and the muscles rippled across his chest and arms when he picked up his towel and dried himself. Their eyes met, making her realise that he was observing her as she was observing him, and she turned her back on him abruptly to dry her own body, but she was still aware of him with every fibre of her being.

Amy did not hear him coming up behind her, but the prickly sensation racing up her spine warned her of his nearness, and she spun round to find him standing no more than a pace away from her. She tried to snatch up her towelling robe, but missed, and she backed a pace away from him instead. His hands were holding the ends of his towel, and his eyes glittered with mockery as he whipped it over her head, catching her firmly about the waist before she had time to take evasive action.

'Come here!' he growled, pulling her up against him, and launching a violent attack on her senses when she felt his naked, male flesh against her own.

'No, Luke!' she protested desperately, her hands flat against his rock-hard chest in an attempt to push him away from her, but the towel bit into her waist, moulding her hips and thighs to his, and sending a shaft of feeling through her that made the blood leap faster through her veins. 'Let me go!' she said in a fury born of fear.

'You can't run for ever, Amy,' he pointed out drily.

'I wasn't aware that I was being chased.'

'Liar!' he accused savagely, his eyes blazing down into hers. 'You know damn well there was an eruption between us from the very moment we met, and we haven't stopped being intensely aware of each other.'

'Stop it, Luke!' she pleaded angrily even though she knew it was the truth.

E

'Can you deny that you've been aware of a physical attraction between us?' he demanded bluntly.

'No, but——' She broke off abruptly and gestured helplessly with her hands as every vestige of strength seemed to leave her body. 'Please, Luke, find someone else.'

'I don't happen to want anyone else.' His voice suddenly had all the qualities of a deep caress, and it sent little shivers through her which she could not suppress. 'I can be patient if I have to be,' he added meaningfully, 'and I'll wait for you until you're ready.'

A new wave of anger rose from the depths of her helplessness. 'You'll wait an eternity, because I'll never——'

'Never say never, Amy!' he interrupted her with a warning note in his deep, caressing voice. 'I can feel you trembling against me, and I know I can make you give me what I want, but I would prefer to wait until you give it to me willingly.'

Every nerve and sinew reacted with a clamouring response to his statement, but her mind still refused to accept it. 'I'm not interested in casual sex.'

'There will be nothing casual about it, my dear Amy,' he laughed throatily. 'I can promise you that.'

He lowered his head and, as if to prove his point, his warm mouth trailed slowly and sensually over the ridge of her collarbone, his tongue exploring the sensitive hollows above and below it. The sensations he aroused were like nothing she had ever experienced before, and her heart was pounding so fast that she could scarcely breathe. There was nothing casual about the way she felt. Her feelings were intense and rather frightening, and Luke was also not unaffected by it. His heart was thudding beneath her palms, and he made no attempt to hide the fact that his body was betraying his own desires.

The blood raced through her veins like liquid fire when he cast aside the towel and slid his hands possessively over her hips and smooth thighs. Her bones seemed to melt beneath his touch, and her arms went up of their own volition to circle his neck when at last he set his mouth on hers. There was nothing restrained in his kisses, they were sensual and erotic, and her fingers locked convulsively in his thick mane at the nape of his neck when his hips moved suggestively against hers. Her mind shouted, *Stop*, but her body wanted more, *much* more!

Amy could never recall afterwards how she got on to the lounger, but she was lying on her back with her arms locked tightly about Luke's neck, and they were kissing each other with a hungry, probing urgency as if they were determined to fan the flame of their desire into a raging fire. His hands were warm against her back and her shoulders, and she had lost the will to resist when his hands peeled aside the stretchy material at her breasts. Her nipples hardened beneath his probing caress until the sweet agony of his touch made her moan against his mouth before it left hers to intensify the arousal his fingers had started.

'Oh, Luke, Luke!' His name escaped her on a shuddering sigh of ecstasy, and her hands trailed their own fluttering exploration across his wide shoulders.

Luke trembled against her, his hand sliding down along her body to caress her thigh, but something jarred, and penetrated through the mist of Amy's drugged mind. It was his mother's voice instructing the servants where to serve the lunch, and it shocked both Luke and Amy back to reality.

He released her with an abrupt exclamation of annoyance, and got to his feet while she reached for her towelling robe and put it on with hands that shook with the extent of her emotions. Luke did not remain at her side, but walked a little distance away, keeping his back rigidly turned towards Amy and his mother until he had regained his equilibrium.

God, this is terrible! Amy thought frantically. *If Luke's mother had not been here we might well have ended up making love on this sun lounger, and in broad daylight too!*

Lunch on the patio that Sunday consisted of cold asparagus soup, crayfish salad, and fresh rolls with coffee, biscuits and cheese. It was beautifully prepared and delicious, but Amy was too distracted to enjoy it. Mrs Tanner was talking to her, and Amy was aware of answering her, but every time she raised her glance it seemed to collide with Luke's, and the message in those tawny depths was very clear. He wanted her, and she was convinced that her own eyes were betraying her by flashing back messages which she did not have the power to withhold. The entire situation had suddenly become a nightmare from which she could not escape.

Amy never quite knew how she got through the rest of that afternoon. Luke suggested a swim after lunch, but Amy opted out this time and went upstairs to change out of her swimsuit. That brief respite gave her the opportunity to pull herself together to some extent, but one look at Luke was sufficient to shatter her composure yet again.

'I hope to see you on my next visit to Cape

Town, Amy,' Mrs Tanner expressed her wish when she and Luke accompanied Amy out to her car later that afternoon.

'I shall look forward to our next meeting,' Amy responded, and she meant it sincerely.

'Am I included in that remark?' Luke enquired mischievously, sending a wave of heat into Amy's cheeks, and she chose to ignore him before she made a worse idiot of herself.

'Goodbye, Mrs Tanner,' Amy smiled at the older woman. 'I hope you have a pleasant flight tomorrow.'

She murmured something similar, but much briefer to Luke, and she avoided his probing, eternally mocking glance by getting into her car and driving away from his home.

Amy could not find one acceptable excuse for her behaviour that day. She had foolishly made no attempt to hide her feelings and, as a result, Luke could not be blamed if he was convinced she would allow him further intimacies. She silently cursed Luke for showing her how vulnerable she really was, and she cursed herself for being so weak. It would not happen again, she promised herself fiercely. She was not going to be merely another name the great Luke Tanner could add to his long list of conquests. *Never!*

'Never say never, Amy!' his warning echoed through her mind and, despite her determination not to surrender, she knew just how vulnerable she would be if he should try to seduce her.

Amy had been in her office barely an hour the following Monday morning when Penny entered carrying a magnificent and enormous arrangement of red roses which she placed on the desk for Amy's inspection.

'This was delivered a few minutes ago, and I took the liberty of putting water in the vase before I brought it through to you,' Penny explained a little breathlessly. 'Shall I leave the arrangement here on your desk?'

Amy stared at the perfect blooms in stunned surprise, and it took a moment to register that Penny was awaiting her reply. 'There isn't a space anywhere else large enough to accommodate the arrangement, so it had better stay on my desk.'

'Aren't you going to open the card?' Penny asked curiously when Amy had regained her composure and was calmly continuing with her work.

'Later,' Amy answered abruptly.

'Oh, I get the message,' Penny giggled. 'It's from someone special, and you want to be alone when you read the card.'

Amy looked up sharply. She could cheerfully have thrown something at her secretary at that moment, and Penny knew it. She giggled again as she beat a hasty retreat and she closed the door firmly behind her.

The long-stemmed buds seemed to dominate the room, and Amy felt an unwilling smile pluck at her lips as she stared at them. She did not need to read the card to know the name of the sender. No one else but Luke Tanner would ever think of sending her such an outrageously big arrangement of deep-red roses. It was a flamboyant gesture which spoke volumes, but the words were not the ones she wanted to hear.

She removed the pin with which the small envelope had been attached to the decorative ribbon and lifted the flap of the envelope to extract the card. Luke's bold handwriting leapt out at her, and her heart was thudding heavily against her ribs when she read the message.

I dare not take the risk that you might forget me while I'm away, but I'm convinced you will think of me at least for as long as these roses will last. L.T.

It really was not at all funny, but Amy started to laugh, and she laughed so much that she eventually cried. When, at last, she managed to control herself, she found Penny and her uncle standing in her office, and they were staring at her as if they thought she had gone slightly mad.

'Are you all right?' they asked almost simultaneously, and Amy nodded behind the lacy handkerchief she pressed to her quivering mouth.

'I'm fine,' she sniffed, dabbing at her eyes. 'I think I've come out of exile.'

A glimmer of understanding flashed across Ben Smythe's face, but it was replaced almost instantly by doubt. Penny, of course, had no idea what Amy was talking about, and Amy did not think she could explain it either.

'Make her a strong cup of tea and give her some aspirins,' her uncle instructed Penny before he walked out of the office, and suddenly Amy wanted to cry again.

A strong cup of tea and aspirins! Oh God, if only the problem could be solved with such a simple remedy!

CHAPTER EIGHT

THE arrangements for the tour went ahead with very few hitches, and the list of bookings from local and overseas agencies was growing longer every day. Amy had never before been quite so busy, and most nights she had to take work home with her.

Luke's roses had lasted the entire week, as if he had injected some of his devilish determination into them. Amy could not help thinking about him; she had thought of him often, but the week away from him had also strengthened her to some extent. She had had some time to take a long, hard look at herself, and she knew that she would never be interested in the temporary affair Luke had to offer her.

Amy had to take work home again on Tuesday evening, and she sat working at her kitchen table until after nine that evening before she packed everything away and went to run her bath water. She was tired, she needed to have an early night for a change, and a soak in a hot bath would relax her and ensure a good night's sleep. She had stepped out of the bath and was drying herself almost an hour later when her doorbell rang. She stiffened nervously. Who could possibly be calling on her at this time of night? The doorbell rang again while she hesitated with indecision, and she quickly put on her robe and pushed her feet into soft mules before leaving the bathroom.

'Who is it?' she called through the door.

'It's me, Luke!' came the answer, and Amy took

a moment to steady herself before she unlocked the door and opened it. Despite all her determined efforts this past week, her heart raced at the sight of him. The jacket of his light grey suit was draped over his arm, his tie had been loosened, and something in his rugged features told her it had been a tough week, but the tawny eyes were still very much alive as they trailed over her with that brilliant gleam of mockery in their depths. 'Have I come at an inconvenient time?'

She stood aside for him to enter and answered him with a calmness she was far from experiencing. 'As you see, I'm not exactly dressed to receive visitors, but, if you don't mind waiting, I'll go and change into something decent.'

'You don't have to do that,' he assured her when they entered the lounge, and his glance flicked over her with renewed interest. 'You look very nice and decent just as you are.'

'Don't be silly, Luke, I can't sit around wearing nothing but a——' She halted abruptly, mortified when she realised exactly what she had told him, and the sensuous smile that accompanied his probing glance sent a wave of embarrassed heat surging into her face. 'Why are you here, anyway?' she demanded angrily.

'I flew in from Johannesburg a half-hour ago, and I thought you might take pity on a weary man and offer me a cup of coffee before I go home,' he enlightened her smoothly, flinging his jacket across the back of the cane bench, and removing his tie before he undid yet another shirt button.

'If you're as weary as you say you should have gone straight home,' she argued, suppressing that wave of tender concern which had threatened to engulf her.

'There's no one there to talk to,' he complained.

'Poor, lonely Luke,' she could not resist mocking him. 'A telephone call would have brought any one of several women to your home to talk to you.'

He studied her slim, erect figure in the coral-pink robe with a speculative gleam in his eyes. 'Would you have come?'

'No,' she answered bluntly, and a derisive smile curved his mouth.

'That's why I'm here.'

Amy wished that she could find something clever to say to that, but her tired mind was having difficulty in functioning properly. The only clear thought in her mind at that moment was that she had missed him more than she had allowed herself to believe during the past week, and if she stayed there with him a moment longer she might just be fool enough to show it.

'You'd better sit down before you drop,' she suggested coldly, turning her back on that fatal magnetism he exuded. 'I'll change and make us something to drink.'

She did not wait for him to reply, but escaped into her bedroom and changed into the first things she could lay her hands on, which were brown linen slacks and a lime-green cotton blouse. She caught sight of her shiny nose in the mirror and hastily dabbed a bit of powder on it before adding a touch of colour to her lips. She brushed her hair to make herself look a little more respectable, and only then did she go through to the kitchen to make the coffee.

Luke lay stretched out on the bench when she brought their coffee through to the lounge. She thought for a moment he was asleep, but he sat up at once when she put his cup on the low table close to him. He was tired, she could see it in the shadows beneath his eyes, and in the deep grooves that ran from nose to mouth. He was a man who worked hard and played hard, and she wondered how much longer he could continue at that pace.

The conversation veered towards the business side of their relationship, and that suited Amy perfectly. They discussed the progress she was making with the arrangements for the first tour from Cape Town to Durban, and he told her about his negotiations to erect a Blue Dolphin holiday resort on the reef. It was a nice, comfortable discussion, but Amy should have known that it could not last.

'Did you get the roses I sent you?' he asked, and her body tensed automatically in a defensive action.

'Yes, thank you.'

'Did you think of me?'

'You made sure that I would, didn't you?' she retorted with some annoyance, and he laughed softly.

'I told you in my note that I couldn't take the risk that you might forget me, and I meant it.'

'I should have thought you were accustomed to taking risks.'

'Not with you, Amy. Never with you.' He drew hard on the cigarette he had lit earlier and he crushed the remainder into the ashtray while he studied her intently through a screen of smoke. 'With you I've always had the feeling that if I turned my back, you might be gone.'

Their glances locked in a silent battle in which neither of them wanted to surrender, but Amy felt her defences crumbling one by one, and she knew she had to get away from him before it was too late.

'I'll take these cups through to the kitchen,' she

said, rising to her feet and collecting their empty coffee cups.

'Is that a gentle hint that you want me to leave?' he mocked her, and she stiffened as she straightened to face him.

'It is rather late, Luke, and you're tired,' she stressed the obvious, her features rigid with the effort to control the feelings that were coursing through her.

'And what if I don't want to go?'

Their eyes met and held, and she knew what he was referring to. He wanted to stay with her, he wanted to make love to her, and, God help her, she wanted it too, but she dared not let it happen. If she wanted to walk out of this relationship with her self-respect intact, then she had to be strong, but the way the cups were rattling in her trembling hands did not exactly signify strength.

Without a word, she spun round and marched into the kitchen. She had to get away from him, but she should have known that he would not let her escape so easily. He followed her into the kitchen, and he was directly behind her when she put the cups in the sink.

'Amy, I was only joking,' he explained, reaching for her, but she darted away from him.

'Don't touch me!' she said, her eyes blazing up into his, and her insides shaking in something close to terror.

'For God's sake!' he thundered, a strange whiteness settling about his mouth. 'Stop behaving as if you think I'm planning to rape you, Amy!'

Rape! That word had the same effect as a slap across the face might have had, and she paled. She had never thought of rape. It had been her own response to his advances she had been afraid of, and even now his nearness made her tremble.

'I'm sorry, I—I guess I'm jumpy, or—or something,' she lamely tried to explain her reaction.

'Or something,' he agreed, and this time she did not shy away from the hands that gripped her shoulders. 'Relax, my dear, you're much too tense.'

She could not relax, she dared not, but his hands were moving against her shoulders, gently massaging the tense muscles until they became pliable beneath his fingers. The faint scent of his masculine cologne was stirring her senses, breaking down her resistance, and suddenly she was in his arms.

'Please . . . don't!' she begged in a whisper, but his eyes held hers, and she was like a moth being drawn irresistibly towards a flame which she knew would scorch her wings.

The tip of his tongue teased the corner of her mouth and traced the outline of her lips, and her mouth opened beneath his with a hungry desire which she knew matched his own. She clung to him a little wildly, her body arching towards his with an aching need she had never known before, but just as suddenly she came to her senses. What was she doing? She was letting her love for him overrule one very important factor. Luke was interested in her body alone, and she dared not surrender to this fierce physical need he aroused in her. He would discard her the moment he tired of her, and she would have lost her self-respect along with her heart. She would be hurt again, and this time far worse than before if she allowed this situation to continue. Her mind cried out this warning, but her body was crying out for something else. Engulfed in a wave of panic, she finally found the strength to push Luke away from her.

'*No!*' she cried out with a note of anguish in her voice which she could not disguise. 'Please, Luke! Please, don't do this to me! Go away . . . find someone else . . . *please*!'

Amy had never before been quite so distraught. She had cried out one thing at Luke, while her heart had cried out exactly the opposite, and it felt as if she was being torn in two right down the middle. She stared up into his grim face through a red mist of pain, and then something quite horrifying happened. Stinging tears filled her eyes and spilled from her lashes on to her pale cheeks, and she buried her quivering face in her hands when that first convulsive sob shook through her. She tried to control herself, but she could not and, when Luke pulled her roughly against him, she buried her face against his wide, solid chest and wept like a child.

Luke held her, his hand stroking her hair until her tears had subsided, and although she could not recall at what stage he had offered her his handkerchief, she made good use of it in the mopping-up process.

'I—I'm sorry,' she sniffed apologetically, drying her eyes and blowing her nose on the fine linen. 'I don't usually burst into tears for no reason at all, and especially not in company.'

'I think you have a very good reason, and I wish you would trust me enough to tell me what it is,' Luke contradicted quietly, leading her towards the kitchen chair. 'Sit down, Amy, and if you tell me where you keep your coffee I'll make us some.'

'It's in the blue and white striped tin,' she told him, lowering herself wearily on to the chair, and in no mood at that moment to argue with him.

'Got it,' he said, and Amy sat there watching him a little incredulously while he made coffee. It seemed so strange, and yet it seemed so right that he should be there. *Please, God, my mind is so confused I don't know what I want any more!* A mug of coffee appeared on the table in front of her, and Luke was saying, 'You'd better taste it and tell me if I'd made it too strong.'

'It's fine, thank you,' she answered him after taking a sip, and she was overcome with embarrassment when she became aware of his intense scrutiny. 'Oh, my face must be in a mess!'

'You're beautiful, so sit down and relax!' he instructed, his hand on her shoulder forcing her back into her chair when she would have risen, and he joined her at the table with his mug of coffee.

He was being incredibly kind to her, but he could not have found it very pleasant having a woman weeping all over him, and she felt rather guilty. She owed him some sort of explanation, but how was she going to explain her behaviour to him without revealing her true feelings? The silence lengthened between them, making her feel awkward and tense, and she finally grasped at the first thing that came to mind.

'I'm sorry, Luke,' she said lamely. 'I guess you caught me at a bad time. I've been snowed under with work, and I'm overwrought and tired.'

His rugged features gave her no insight into what he was thinking, or feeling, but there was a quiet conviction in his voice when he said, 'There's more to it than that, isn't there?'

'Oh, Luke!' Her voice was choked with renewed tears, and she passed a weary hand over her red-rimmed eyes. She should have known that he would not rest until he knew it all, and she was not so sure that she was ready to tell him everything. 'What do you want of me, Luke?' she demanded tiredly.

'I want to know everything, Amy.' His compelling glance drew hers and held it. 'I have reason to believe you're a warm, passionate woman. You possess emotional depths that are as yet unexplored, but for some reason you're afraid of it, and you reject it. I want to know why, and I want to know what caused it.'

It was a quiet command that left her with no choice at all, but still she prevaricated. 'It's a long story, and we're both tired.'

'Tell me, Amy.'

It was an order now, and for the first time in four years she found herself talking about the incidents which had almost shattered her own life. It was difficult at first, and her voice faded into silence on several occasions, but she forced herself to continue. She told him everything she had kept locked away inside her for so long, and it felt as if she was slowly cleansing a festering wound when at last she told him of the months of therapy which had ended her ordeal.

Luke's hand closed over hers, the pressure of his fingers comforting as he carried her hand to his lips, but he said nothing. He did not have to when his eyes looked into hers with insight and complete understanding.

'Oh God, Luke!' She dragged her fingers from his to bury her quivering face in her hands for a moment. 'It hurts too much when you lose the people you care about. That's why I don't want to get involved, because I don't want to learn to care again only to be hurt.'

Luke did not respond to this at once, and neither did she want him to. They drank their coffee in silence, each busy with their own thoughts, and it was only when Luke took their empty mugs and placed them in the sink that he confronted her with his opinion.

'What you've told me proves my theory. You're a sensitive woman, and you feel things deeply. When you care about someone it's a deep and all-time commitment, and when they're gone it's a loss too deep to overcome lightly. Not many people have the ability to feel that way, but there is always a bright as well as a darker side to life, Amy, and we must learn to accept the bad with the good.' He lowered his gaze to her hands laced so tightly together on the table, and he covered them both with one large hand. 'You can't spend the rest of your life shutting yourself away from a closer relationship with people simply because you're afraid to face up to reality.'

Amy's face went a shade paler. Uncle Ben had said something similar often enough in the past, but it was a great deal more shattering to hear Luke put it into words, and her gaze fell before his. 'I know I'm a coward, but I can't help it.'

'I think you're a woman of great courage,' he corrected, his grip tightening on her hands which were still locked so firmly together. 'It takes courage to choose to walk a solitary path through life, and it also takes courage to break down those protective and impenetrable barriers you've erected around yourself, but you can do it, and I know you will.'

She digested this in silence, but she would analyse her feelings later. She could not think straight at that moment, it had simply been a relief to talk, and now she needed time alone to sort herself out.

Luke got up to leave almost as if he sensed her desire to be alone, and she followed him when he walked into the lounge to collect his jacket and tie.

'Thanks for listening, Luke,' she said tiredly when they reached the door, and he tipped her face up to his.

For seemingly endless seconds he looked down into her dark, haunted eyes. 'You're not going to get rid of me so easily, and you might as well accept that as a fact.' He lowered his head and kissed her firmly on the lips. 'Good night, Amy.'

The flat was as silent and empty as Amy felt after Luke had gone. She was drained of all emotion when she switched off the lights and went to bed, and it was when she lay staring into the darkness that she realised she was still clutching Luke's handkerchief in her hand. She would have to launder it before she returned it to him, but for the moment it comforted her to have something of his with her, and she slipped it under her pillow and promptly went to sleep.

Amy felt curiously light after unburdening herself to Luke but she was also infinitely more wary. She could not explain why, but she had the odd sensation that she had torn off her armour, and suddenly she was naked and totally vulnerable.

Luke telephoned her at the office on the Thursday of that same week, and the sound of his deep voice in her ear quickened her pulse.

'Will you have dinner with me this evening, Amy?' he invited, and he did not wait for her to accept or reject his invitation. 'Wear something casual,' he suggested, 'preferably slacks.'

Amy was instantly on the alert. 'Is this an invitation to your home, Luke?'

'No,' came the abrupt reply. 'I'm taking you to a place where you'll be so close to the sea you could almost dip your fingers in the water while we're having dinner.'

'You're making me curious,' she confessed.

'Good!' he said in that same abrupt manner. 'I'll call for you at seven.'

The line went dead, and a slight frown creased her smooth brow when she slowly replaced the receiver on its cradle. Where on earth did Luke intend taking her, and where could she be so close to the sea that she could dip her fingers in the water while having dinner?

She spent several puzzled moments considering this, then she shrugged it off and buzzed her secretary to come in and take dictation.

Luke arrived at her flat at exactly seven o'clock that evening, and five minutes later they were speeding towards the city in his Ferrari. They turned south, however, before they reached the city, and he took the road towards Muizenberg.

Amy's curiosity was increasing, and she could no longer restrain herself when they had passed Fish Hoek and were heading towards Simonstown. 'Where are we going?'

'Be patient a little while longer, Amy,' he smiled, negotiating a bend in the road. 'We're almost there.'

Amy was more than a little confused when he turned off towards the harbour in Simonstown and parked his car on the docks. Luke helped her out and locked the Ferrari's doors before taking her hand and leading her towards a pier along which several yachts were moored. It was almost dark, but the harbour was well lit where they stopped beside one of the larger yachts. It was sleek and white and powerful-looking, and Amy's curiosity increased. The yacht swayed in the slight swell of the ocean, and so did the narrow gangplank as Luke led the way across it and leapt silently on to the deck in his canvas shoes.

'Welcome aboard the *Amazon*, Amy,' he smiled faintly, taking her hand and helping her on to the scrubbed deck, and she had never been more thankful that she had chosen to wear soft-soled, rope sandals with her slacks and sweater. 'I use her as a bolt-hole when I need to escape the pressure of work.'

Any steadied herself on her feet while her sweeping, rather bewildered glance took in the tall masts, and the spotless deck with its gleaming rails. 'We're having dinner on your yacht?'

'Novel idea, don't you agree?' His tawny eyes glittered down into hers as if he found her bewilderment amusing. 'Come on, let me show you around.'

There were two luxury staterooms below deck with four smaller cabins, and all the amenities of a home. On a level with the deck was the main saloon. It was like a large room with green velvet curtains drawn aside at the windows, wood-panelling on the walls, and concealed lighting. The only visible indication that they were on a yacht was the fact that the comfortably padded benches and chairs were bolted to the carpeted floor. The bar was pure artistry in solid mahogany, and it acted as a divider between the living and dining areas.

'Very impressive,' Amy answered the silent query in Luke's eyes, but the next instant her face paled and she was clutching at the back of the chair beside her. 'What's happening? Why are the engines starting up?'

'Don't panic,' Luke announced blandly. 'I gave the crew instructions to take us a short distance beyond the harbour.'

'You never said anything about going out to sea!'

Her voice was a nervous squeak as she stood there clutching at the chair while the *Amazon*'s powerful engines propelled them away from the pier . . . and safety.

'Relax, Amy.'

Relax? She was suddenly so tense that she would snap like a reed in a strong breeze, and how could she relax while he stood there looking like a satanic pirate in his blue denims, and red and white striped sweater. Luke raised a heavy eyebrow in mocking appraisal, then he walked towards the bar, and the sound of glass touching glass jarred her raw nerve ends.

She seated herself gingerly on the chair she had been clutching before her legs caved in beneath her, and the heavy beat of her heart seemed to be keeping time with the rhythmic throbbing of the *Amazon*'s engines.

'Drink this,' Luke instructed, placing a glass between her trembling fingers, and she stared suspiciously at its contents.

'What is it?'

'Gin and tonic.' His mouth twitched with the suggestion of a smile as he seated himself on a chair close to hers. 'That's what you usually drink when you're nervous and feel threatened, isn't it?'

Amy stiffened at his mockery, her heart beating in her throat. 'Don't I have reason to feel nervous and threatened?'

'Perhaps,' he smiled lazily, his glance faintly insolent as it roamed over her slender body clad in an apricot-coloured sweater and white slacks which did not hide her feminine curves while alarm bells started ringing in her mind.

'If you think——'

'I don't think, Amy, I know,' he interrupted calmly, swallowing a mouthful of his drink and watching her intently.

'If you try anything, Luke, I—I swear I'll——'

'You swear you'll *what*, my dear?' he prompted when her voice faded into a choked silence.

She wrenched her glance from his and gulped down a mouthful of her gin and tonic to steady her nerves. She was getting panicky when it would be safer to remain calm.

'Don't do this to me, Luke,' she pleaded, trying to decide whether he was serious, or simply baiting her for his own amusement.

'I haven't done anything to you . . . yet.'

'But you're planning to, aren't you?'

He looked into her anxious, honey-brown eyes and laughed unexpectedly. 'Amy, you're the most suspicious woman I've ever met, and I've met plenty.'

'You don't have to remind me of your long list of conquests,' she retorted, her distaste evident.

'Does it make you jealous?' he teased her.

'Most certainly not!' she lied, feigning indignation, but the low rumble of his laughter made her suspect that she had not fooled him one iota.

The yacht's engines were cut abruptly, and the silence that followed was almost deafening. Amy once again had to fight down her rising panic, and in the process she drained her glass.

'We've dropped anchor, and if you look out of the porthole to the starboard side you will see the lights of Simonstown quite clearly.' Luke's mocking glance met hers. 'They're close enough to give you sufficient light to swim ashore if you're too afraid to be alone with me.'

'That isn't funny, Luke!' she snapped angrily.

'I agree.'

She could not detect a trace of mockery on his face at that moment, and for some obscure reason she knew suddenly that she was in no danger at all.

'I suppose you think I've been behaving like an idiot.'

'I wouldn't say that,' he contradicted, 'but you were over-reacting a little.'

'I'm sorry.'

'You're forgiven,' he smiled, a teasing light in his eyes as he gestured to her glass. 'You swallowed that drink so fast I'm convinced it never touched the sides.'

'You could always pour me another,' she suggested, relaxing in her chair as the tension slowly eased out of her body.

'It will be a pleasure,' Luke announced, taking her glass from her and rising to his feet.

It was a warm night with a crescent moon in a sky where a million stars were clustered together, and in the silence Amy could hear the water lapping against the sides of the yacht as it swayed and rolled gently. The night was too perfect to mar with foolish fears.

Their dinner was served some time later by the coloured chef Amy had glimpsed earlier in the galley down below. It took two trips to carry everything up on trays, from their prawn cocktails to their coffee, then he bowed himself out and left them alone to help themselves.

Marinated steak with mushrooms and vegetables followed the prawn dish, and the mouthwatering aroma made Amy realise how hungry she actually was. She had had a slice of toast and coffee for breakfast, and she had been too busy to bother about lunch, but this meal on the *Amazon* had been worth starving herself for.

'I'm going to Johannesburg again tomorrow,' Luke sprang the news on her while they were eating. 'I'm leaving on the early morning flight.'

The succulent steak turned to leather in her mouth, and she swallowed it with difficulty. 'How long will you be away?'

'Are you asking because you think you might miss me?' he teased, hitting the mark with a frightening accuracy.

'I'm asking because I'd like you to be present when we send off the first coachload of tourists with a champagne breakfast,' she disillusioned him, and he grimaced.

'I arrive back the day before the tour departs,' he set her mind at rest, but not her heart.

'That's perfect.'

'I'll be away for ten days.'

'I know,' she answered casually, spearing a small piece of steak and popping it into her mouth.

'You could at least tell me you'll miss me!' he growled accusingly, impaling her on her chair with his narrowed glance.

'Oh, Luke, you're impossible!' she sighed, putting down her knife and her fork and studying him across the candlelit table with a mixture of amusement and annoyance dancing in her warm, honey-brown eyes. 'Since the day you walked into my life you've turned everything upside down and inside out, and I don't quite know what to do about it.'

A dangerous glint entered his eyes. 'Shall I tell you what to do about it?'

'No,' she shook her head, knowing exactly what he would suggest. 'It's something I have to sort out for myself.'

'The trouble with you is you're stubborn and too confoundedly independent,' he accused, attacking what was left of his food.

'I acknowledge the fact that I have an independent streak, but I'm not stubborn,' she argued, picking up her knife and fork and continuing her meal.

'Old-fashioned, then,' he corrected abruptly.

'Is that such a bad thing?'

'For me it is!' he announced with a hint of savagery in his voice. 'I'm a man with a normal, healthy sex drive, but since meeting you I've been living the life of a celibate, and I don't like it.'

Her cheeks went hot, and she lowered her lashes hastily. 'I've told you often enough to find someone else, Luke.'

'And I've told you that I don't want anyone else!' he countered somewhat harshly.

'In that case I can only offer you my sympathy,' she mocked him, and her lashes swept up the next instant at the sound of his deep-throated laughter.

'You're as hard as nails, Amy,' he informed her when his laughter subsided, 'but I'm damned if I shall give up.'

That's what she was afraid of! If he persisted, then she might eventually relent, and that would lead her nowhere except towards disillusionment and pain. The only good thing that had come out of their relationship, was that he had done her the favour of making her face reality again, but her love for him was something she would simply have to overcome.

Brave words! her mind jeered. Her love for this man was not something she would be capable of brushing off like an unwelcome speck of dust from her clothes. It was there, it was alive, and it would remain a part of her life until the end of her days. *Oh, God, why did I have to fall in love with a man who could never offer me more than a temporary place in his life!*

CHAPTER NINE

AMY'S hands rested lightly on the rail as she stood beside Luke and stared out across the restless ocean rippling in the moonlight. The air was fresh and salty, and she breathed it into her lungs to let it out on a sigh.

'It's peaceful, isn't it?' Luke spoke softly into the silence.

'Yes, it is,' she agreed, a smile curving her soft mouth as she looked up into his shadowed face.

He leaned with his back against the rail, trailing his fingers up the length of her arm, and the thousand little nerves leapt as usual to attention at his touch. 'I wish you could come to Johannesburg with me.'

'And what would I do all day while you're involved in your business negotiations?' she questioned him with a calmness which did not quite match the sensations his touch was arousing.

'You could spend your days shopping, and at night we could go out to dinner, or the theatre, and . . . who knows?'

'And how lovely that would look splashed all over the newspapers,' she pointed out mockingly, trying to ignore those strong fingers sliding across her shoulder and beneath her hair to caress the nape of her neck.

'We'll be very discreet,' he promised with a wicked gleam in his eyes as he moved closer to her.

'With a man in your position that simply isn't possible,' she argued, the pleasure of his touch sending receptive little shivers racing along her spine. 'Wherever you go, and whatever you do, you're news. The media will never leave you entirely alone,' she added, the clean male smell of him alerting her senses to the danger of his nearness.

'I could always lock you up in my suitcase and sneak you into my hotel bedroom,' he suggested.

'That's what I'm afraid of,' she laughed softly, and she was instantly aware of a new tension building up between them.

'Has anyone ever told you you've got a sexy laugh?'

'Don't be silly!' She turned away from him, escaping his touch, but she was aware of him following her across the deck and into the main saloon, and she glanced nervously at her watch. 'Isn't it about time we returned to the harbour?'

'The night is still young, Amy.'

'It's after eleven.'

'And in forty-five minutes' time it will be the bewitching hour of midnight,' he mocked her.

'I'm not staying here until that time,' she protested.

'I'm afraid you have no choice.'

'What do you mean?' she demanded, spinning round to face him and finding herself looking a long way up into his mocking eyes.

'The crew took the dinghy ashore while we were having our dinner, and they have orders not to return until midnight.'

Her heart was beating so hard and fast that she could scarcely breathe. Should she panic, or was he merely baiting her? 'I imagine you had a very good reason for issuing those instructions?'

'I like my privacy, and I wanted to be alone with you.'

'Should I feel threatened?' she warily asked the

same question she had voiced earlier that evening, and his smile sent a weakness into her limbs.

'I've never taken a woman against her will, Amy,' he said, framing her face with his hands. 'Hang on to that thought, will you?'

His rugged features became a blur when he lowered his head and set his mouth on hers. Her lips parted with an eagerness she despised herself for, but she could not still that growing hunger for his kisses. The probing intimacy of his tongue was intoxicating, and her thudding heartbeat silenced the voice of her conscience. Her hands slid from his waist across his back to cling to his broad shoulders, and her body relaxed against his as hidden fires came to life inside her.

Amy was trembling when he eased himself away from her. She was incapable of thinking clearly as she blindly allowed him to lead her from the saloon, and down into his stateroom below. It was when she saw the double bunk with its blue, satin quilt that she came painfully to her senses, but Luke was lifting her in his arms, and walking purposefully towards the bunk.

'No, Luke!' she begged in a strangled voice as she struggled in his arms, but his arms were like steel bands clamped about her, and he lowered her on to the quilted bunk to hold her there with his hard body.

'Be still, Amy,' he murmured soothingly, his hand caressing her smooth, flushed cheek and her hair as if she were a child. 'Be still, my love.'

My love? That stilled her as nothing else could have done. Those two words could have meant so little to him that he may have uttered them without actually being aware of it, but her heart quickened its pace in response, and a glowing warmth flowed through her that left her pliant in his arms.

Luke kissed the warm hollow at the base of her throat, and she could almost feel her pulse beating against his mouth before it travelled slowly across her throat to create delicious havoc with her emotions. She closed her eyes and arched her neck, inviting the exploration of his mouth and the fiery sensations it aroused. When at last his mouth found hers she was seared by the white-hot passion of his kiss. It seemed to burn deep into her soul to awaken a quivering need, and she locked her arms about his neck in abject surrender.

His thigh lay heavy across her own, and his hands were beneath her sweater, leaving a burning trail of sensuous fire against her soft, responsive flesh. She was beginning to feel light-headed with desire, and although her mind still issued a warning, it was becoming fainter with every passing second. The catch of her bra gave way beneath Luke's fingers, and his hands brushed aside the lacy cups to clasp her breasts. His light touch against the sensitive peaks aroused her to the exquisite agony of a desire she had never known before, and she could not suppress the moan of pleasure that spilled from her lips.

Amy was clutching a little wildly at his shoulders when he pushed up her sweater to expose her breasts to his hot, seeking mouth, and her breath came in little gasps of pleasure when his lips and his tongue continued the erotic arousal until her nipples were hard, aching buttons of desire.

'You're so soft, and so beautiful, Amy,' he groaned, burying his face in the scented hollow between her breasts. 'And wanting you is driving me nearly out of my mind.'

Wanting you, wanting you! His words echoed through her mind as if they had been shouted into a hollow chamber, and sanity returned like a glass of iced water which had been flung into her face when Luke eased himself away from her. Her eyes were wide and dark in her pale face as she stared up at him, and a wave of shame engulfed her at the knowledge that it was Luke who had brought this moment of madness to an end because of the tight rein he had kept on his desire for her. If the decision had been left up to *her* there would have been no turning back, and she was having difficulty in digesting this shattering discovery.

'God help me, Luke, I'm sorry, but I——'

'I know, you're not yet prepared to let me make love to you,' he interrupted her with a twisted smile, misconstruing her horrified attempt at an apology for her abandoned behaviour. 'I guess I'll have to marry you first,' he added coals to that fire of shame which was spreading so rapidly through her.

'I don't want marriage! I don't want anything, I——' She pushed him away with a choked cry and sat up with her back to him to fasten the clasp of her bra and pull down her sweater. *I guess I'll have to marry you first!* Oh, what a mockery! Marriage was the last thing in the world he wanted. He wanted her body with no strings attached, and she would have given herself to him with a shameless eagerness. 'Isn't it midnight yet?' she asked, combing her fingers through her dishevelled hair and getting to her feet without looking at him.

At that very moment the engines started throbbing, and Luke's mocking voice said behind her, 'It's midnight.'

They left the stateroom and went up on deck to the main saloon. Luke poured a whisky for himself, and a gin and tonic for Amy which she did not refuse. She needed something strong to settle the tremors which still coursed through her body, and she sipped her drink while she stared at the lights of the harbour coming steadily closer.

The *Amazon* was moored securely, and Luke gave Amy a hand up on to the swaying gangplank. They stepped on to the pier and walked in silence to his car. She felt him looking at her, willing her to say something, but her jaw was clenched so tightly she could not speak even if she had wanted to.

'Take it easy, my dear,' he said, his hand finding hers in the darkness when he got behind the wheel of the Ferrari. 'Nothing happened, and nothing *will*, if that's the way you want it.'

Shut up! she wanted to scream at him. *Don't you realise that I'm ashamed of the fact that it was your restraint and not mine that saved me from losing my self-respect this evening?*

Luke started the car and drove away, and neither of them spoke during the drive to her flat. Amy felt that she owed him an apology, and she was trying to formulate the words in her mind, but everything she thought of seemed so totally inadequate that she discarded it again in search for something else.

He was saying good night to her at her flat, and still she had not found the right words to express her shame, but she had to make an attempt.

'Luke, I'd like to——'

His finger against her lips silenced her. 'I'll see you in ten days' time.'

He turned on his heel and walked out of her flat, and Amy sagged against the wall, closing her eyes against those ridiculous tears that suddenly threatened to spill from her lashes.

*   *   *

Ben Smythe was sitting in Amy's office a week later when Amy's secretary burst into her office without knocking.

'Amy, I've got——' Penny broke off abruptly at the sight of the man seated there, and backed again towards the door. 'Sorry, Mr Smythe.'

'Come in, Penny,' he smiled. 'We weren't discussing anything private and confidential.'

'We've got a problem,' Penny explained, approaching Amy's desk more sedately this time. 'The guide for Monday's coastal tour has been admitted to hospital with acute appendicitis, and we don't have anyone else at such short notice.'

Amy felt a stab of anxiety. 'What happened to the guide we had on stand-by?'

'I'm afraid I gave instructions to fire him last week when complaints came in that he was drinking and using obscene language on the peninsula tours,' Uncle Ben enlightened her ruefully.

'Damn!' A frown creased Amy's brow. 'Have you telephoned all the agencies, Penny?'

'I have,' Penny nodded, her eyes as wide and anxious as Amy felt. 'At this short notice they have no one available.'

Amy tapped her pen agitatedly against the blotter on her desk. There was a solution to this problem. She could take charge of the tour, but could she leave her uncle alone with the masses of work coming in of late?

'There's only one person I know of who is capable of taking that coastal tour on the road,' Ben Smythe announced, and when Amy raised her frowning glance she found him studying her intently. 'You could do it, Amy.'

'I've though of that,' she admitted without hesitation, 'but what about you, Uncle Ben?'

'I'll cope,' he assured her, and both Amy and Penny heaved a silent sigh of relief.

The tour would go on the road as planned, and Amy could only pray that there would be no further hitches.

The champagne breakfast to launch the first tour was a wonderful idea to get everyone acquainted that Monday morning, and the party was in a jovial mood as the time neared for them to depart from Cape Town's Blue Dolphin hotel. Luke was there. Amy had seen him, but not to speak to, and it was almost time for the coach to leave when he walked across the restaurant towards her and placed a firm, detaining hand on her shoulder.

'Keep this evening free for me, will you?'

'I'm afraid I can't,' she said, her pulse quickening at his nearness and, before she could explain, Uncle Ben rose to his feet, and addressed the twenty-eight visitors seated at the long table.

'Ladies and gentlemen, I'm afraid we had an unfortunate hitch at the last minute.' A distressed murmur arose, but Ben Smythe raised his hand to silence them. 'Your leader on this tour has landed himself in hospital with appendicitis, but there's no cause for alarm. The person I have assigned to you has far better qualifications. She is my partner, Amy Warren.'

There was loud hand-clapping as Ben Smythe pointed Amy out to the group, but Amy was aware only of Luke's narrowed, angry eyes resting on her face.

'You're taking this tour on the road?'

'There was no one else,' she explained, and his mouth tightened.

'Dammit, Amy, when am I going to see you again?'

F

'In Durban in two weeks' time when we send off the next group with a similar gesture to this morning's,' she answered him lightly, but her heart was heavy when she walked away from him and announced that the coach was ready to leave.

The luxury, air-conditioned coach with the Aloe emblem on its sides was pulling away from the entrance of the hotel some minutes later. The passengers waved enthusiastically, Luke and Ben Smythe waved back, and soon they were moving through the city traffic. They took the road to Mossel Bay where they would spend the first night of this tour, but there would be several stops in between to visit places of scenic and historic interest.

Amy had little time to relax on the trip. It was a demanding tour that required her complete concentration at all times, and the little free time she had was spent telephoning ahead to check and confirm the planned itinerary. The group responded with an enthusiasm which was rewarding, and Amy could not in all honesty say that she had not enjoyed doing the tour.

Luke was constantly in her thoughts, and she could not help thinking about the time they had done this trip together. She longed to see him again even though she was afraid of it, and she wondered if he would still be angry with her when they met in Durban.

The weather was hot and humid on the last leg of the tour from Margate to Durban, and Amy was exhausted when they arrived at the hotel on Sunday morning before lunch. Janet Hawkins was there to welcome them, and it was only when everyone else had been allocated a room that Janet gave Amy the key to the suite she had occupied on her previous visit with Luke.

'There must be some mistake,' Amy protested. 'A room with a bathroom will do.'

'This suite was allocated to you, and it was done on Luke's instructions,' Janet insisted, and Amy was too tired to argue. 'Will you join us for lunch?'

Amy shook her head wearily. 'If you don't mind, I'd prefer to have sandwiches and tea sent up to the suite, and then I simply want to sleep.'

'All right, my dear,' Janet smiled. 'Luke should also be here any minute now, and ... speak of the devil!'

Amy turned to see Luke striding towards them, and Janet walked into his embrace as if she belonged there. Jealousy, unexpected and all-consuming, took possession of Amy, and she felt her insides starting to shake.

'It's good to see you again, Janet,' Luke was saying, his arm lingering about Janet's waist when he turned to Amy and smiled. 'Hello, Amy.'

'Good morning,' she responded stiffly and rather coldly, and his eyebrows rose a fraction above his mocking eyes.

'Is that how you welcome me?'

'I'm tired, and I'm going up to my suite,' she enlightened him, an icy anger sweeping up a storm inside her. 'Please excuse me.'

Amy picked up her bag and walked away from them to press the lift button. Mercifully the lift doors slid open at once, and she stepped into the steel cage in a fuming temper. How *could* he? she asked herself while the lift swept her up to the twenty-fourth floor at a sickening pace. How *dare* he imagine that she would be foolish enough to agree to any kind of relationship with him when he was making it obvious that he was still in love with Janet Hawkins after all these years!

Jealousy was a terrible thing, Amy discovered to

her dismay. It warped the mind, and gnawed away at her like a cancer. She ordered sandwiches and tea, but she was barely conscious of consuming them. She was hot and tired and, stripping down to her bra and panties, she stretched out on the bed and went to sleep almost immediately.

She slept deeply, her dreams a confused jumble of what had occurred since her departure from Cape Town two weeks ago, but Luke was there too, and so was Janet, and Amy was being tormented.

She awoke with a start several hours later to find Luke leaning against the door jamb between the bedroom and the lounge. An odd little smile was playing about his strong, sensuous mouth, and suddenly she realised why. She snatched at the bedspread and draped it about her as she sat up in bed with a jerk.

'What are you doing here?' she demanded sharply, her cheeks flaming with embarrassment.

'You have a beautiful body, Amy,' he assured her smoothly, pushing himself away from the door and walking towards her with a look in his eyes that made her squirm uncomfortably. 'Why do you want to hide it?'

'How did you get in?' she snapped, ignoring his query.

His hand went into the pocket of his grey slacks and emerged with a key dangling at the end of a silver chain. 'I have a skeleton key to all the rooms.'

'You had no right to walk into my room without knocking!' she accused furiously, dragging the bedspread closer about her.

'I did knock, but when there was no answer I thought that you might be ill,' he explained, watching her closely. 'You looked a bit odd when I arrived, and I was concerned.'

I was jealous because I happen to love you, but that wouldn't mean a thing to you, would it? The words hovered precariously on her lips, but she bit them back hastily. 'I'm in perfect health, now do you mind getting out so that I can get dressed?' she said icily.

'I like you just the way you are,' Luke smiled, his glance resting on her bare shoulders as he seated himself on the bed beside her, and panic mingled with her anger.

'Go away, Luke!'

He studied her intently, his mouth tightening, then he changed the subject. 'We're having dinner with Janet and Garth this evening.'

The last thing Amy wanted was to sit at the same table with Luke and Janet, and her sympathies were entirely with poor, gentle Garth.

'Make my apologies, I'm not hungry,' she said coldly, and a flicker of anger erupted in the tawny eyes regarding her so closely.

'Dammit, Amy, what's the matter with you!' he demanded harshly. 'I got a cool reception from you when I arrived earlier, and now you're positively frozen. What the hell is going on?'

'Nothing is going on, and you're imagining things.'

'I'm not insensitive, and I don't have that kind of imagination,' he argued in a clipped voice. 'What's the matter with you?'

'Nothing!' she snapped, his nearness attacking her senses and straining her nerves to breaking point. 'Go away and leave me alone!'

His hands gripped her shoulders, the pressure of his fingers an agony as well as an ecstasy. 'Stop that, Amy! I'm losing patience with you!'

'Let go of me!' she ordered, trying to shake off his hands without losing her grip on the bedspread and failing. 'Go away!'

'My God, Amy, I won't have you talking to me like that!' he warned, a strange whiteness appearing about his mouth. 'Take care that you don't drive me too far!'

'Leave me alone!' she stormed at him, temporarily blind to the visible signs of danger. 'Go away and find someone else, but for God's sake, leave me in peace!'

Luke did not react at once, then a frightening anger distorted his rugged features. His fingers bit painfully deep into her soft flesh, and he thrust her from him to get to his feet.

'You asked for this, remember that!' he bit out the words with a savagery she had never seen in him before, and her eyes widened with horror when she saw him pull off his white sweater and remove his shoes and socks.

'What are you doing?' she croaked, her eyes wide and dark in her white face, and her heart beating in her throat like a terrified bird, but she knew the answer without being told.

'I'm going to teach you a lesson you're not going to forget in a hurry!' his voice grated across her raw nerves, and she felt the chill of ice sliding into her veins when his hands went to the buckle of his belt.

'No, Luke!' she pleaded, incapable of taking her eyes off his hands undoing that buckle. 'No . . . please!'

'You brought this on yourself,' he reminded her harshly. 'Now you'll have to suffer the consequences.'

'Luke, I—I didn't mean what—what I said,' she stammered helplessly, shrinking up against the padded headboard as an icy fear rushed through her.

'You meant it all right!' he said through his teeth as he pulled down the zip of his slacks.

Fear was beginning to choke her, and her hands were shaking as she clutched the bedspread about her. She had to get away from him and, leaping off the bed, she darted for the door.

'Oh no, my dear, there will be no running away,' he laughed satanically, moving with the speed and agility of a jungle cat.

The unexpected weight of his foot on the trailing point of the bedspread was sufficient to bring her down on to the floor in an ungainly heap, and before she could move she was scooped up into Luke's arms as if she weighed nothing at all.

Naked, except for her flimsy undies, she kicked and beat at his chest and shoulders with her fists. *'Let me go!'* she screamed frantically.

'I'll let you go when it suits me, and not before!' he informed her, flames of fury leaping in his tawny eyes as he flung her on to the bed and held her there with his hard body.

'No!' she cried out, choked with fear as she tried to fight him off, but he held her down effortlessly with one hand while the other stripped her with a total disregard for the lacy garments he was ripping to shreds in the process. 'Don't, Luke . . . please . . . *don't!'*

His laughter cut across her pleas, and terror renewed her strength. She fought him but it simply heightened his desire instead of diminishing it. Amy's flailing hands were pinned helplessly above her head, and her breath was rasping in her throat as she glared up at Luke. She hated him at this moment, and she would never forgive him, but hidden fires threatened to erupt deep down inside her as the length of his hard, male body shifted over hers. *Damn!* She was *not* going to surrender lightly. If he forced himself on her it would be rape, but as his warm mouth descended a shudder of ecstasy rippled through her body.

Oh God! she thought frantically when her treacherous body stilled beneath his. *It isn't going to be rape!*

His mouth sought hers, and she turned her head away as a last, defiant attempt to resist him, but he pulled her face towards his setting his mouth on hers and forcing her lips apart.

There was no escape from the punishment he intended to mete out, but somehow he stirred to life an incredible excitement that drove everything from her mind except the taste and feel of him. Their bodies clung with the dampness of perspiration, and Amy was beyond caring when his hands trailed down her quivering, receptive body in search of the most intimate part of her. There was a strange new fire in her blood as it raced through her veins, and her body arched unashamedly towards his, welcoming the intimacy of his touch.

'Oh, Luke, Luke!' she heard herself gasping his name in a voice she barely recognised as her own, and her hands were clutching at his muscled back, drawing him closer as her need spiralled higher. She loved him, she wanted him, and suddenly nothing else mattered beyond that. She was his to do with as he pleased, but, at that precise moment of complete surrender, Luke broke away from her and got up. Confused and completely bewildered, she saw him pick up his clothes and put them on. *What was he doing? What had she done that was wrong?* She pushed herself up on to her elbows and stared at him.

'Luke, what's wrong?'

'I've changed my mind,' he said in a cold, abrupt voice, picking up the bedspread and flinging it across her body.

'You can't leave me, Luke!' She stared at him, dismayed and incredulous. 'Not now!'

He had zipped himself into his slacks, and he pulled on his sweater before he stepped towards the bed and leaned over her with his hands pressing into the bed on either side of her. 'Is your body aching for mine, Amy?'

She had gone beyond the desire for subterfuge as she looked up into his unfathomable eyes, and the truth spilled from her swollen, throbbing lips. 'Yes!' she answered him, her eyes still dark and stormy with the force of the emotions he had aroused. 'I want you . . . *please!*'

'Good!' he snarled at her, reaching for his shoes and socks and putting them on. 'Now you know the kind of hell I've been going through these past two months.'

'Luke!'

'I'm leaving you alone, Amy,' he smiled derisively into the pale, pinched face raised to his. 'That's what you wanted, and that's what you're going to get!'

He turned on his heel and strode out of her suite, slamming the door behind him with a force that made her flinch violently.

Amy sat up, clutching the bedspread around her, shaking so much that her teeth were chattering. She was cold, her skin felt icy and clammy, but it was nothing compared with the pain of the iciness shifting slowly through her body to douse the fire of that aching need Luke had aroused. She could not believe what had happened. It was like a nightmare, but the reality of it was an agony such as she had never known in her pain-filled life.

Damn Luke! *Damn* him for what he had done to her! And *damn* him for the humiliation of leading her to that insane pitch of desire where she had actually begged him to take her! She would *never* forgive him for that!

Humiliation, wave after sickening wave of it, swept the heat back into her shivering body. She stormed into the shower and she opened the cold water tap so that the fierce jet of water pummelled her bruised flesh in an attempt to erase the memory of Luke's hands on her body.

The new batch of tourists was assembled in the hotel restaurant on Monday morning when Amy walked in. The champagne breakfast had been served, the conversation flowed as they got to know each other, and the leader on this tour was an eager-faced young man who could scarcely wait to get the tour on the road to Cape Town.

Amy's glance collided with Luke's across the restaurant, and her heart lurched violently in her breast. His eyes seemed to burn their way through her, and inherent politeness made her incline her head in a silent greeting, but he turned his back on her without acknowledging it, and smiled down at Janet Hawkins who was speaking to him.

He had snubbed her, cutting her to the quick, and Amy's cheeks flamed before the blood receded from her face to leave her deathly pale.

She never quite knew afterwards how she managed to smile pleasantly during the address she had had to deliver on behalf of Aloe Tours. She could not recall at what time during the proceedings she realised that Luke was no longer there and, when she stood outside the hotel waving off the coachload of passengers, it was Garth Hawkins who informed her that Luke had left for the airport some time ago. He had gone without saying goodbye!

If he had wanted to hurt her, then he had succeeded only too well, but in retrospect she found herself admitting that she had only herself to blame for it.

'I'm leaving you alone, Amy,' he had said before he had stormed out of her suite. 'That's what you wanted, and that's what you're going to get!'

Yes, that was what she had said she wanted, but in her heart she had wanted something quite different. She had wanted his love, but his love had been given elsewhere a long time ago. She had stoically refused him access to her body, but he had rejected her when she had finally offered herself to him.

'Now you know the kind of hell I've been going through these past two months,' Luke's snarling voice echoed in her mind.

That was true! He had aroused a fierce hunger in her body, and leaving it unfulfilled had been an agony she had not recovered from easily. Mentally she had also gone through a private hell of her own, but his snubbing her and leaving Durban that morning without saying goodbye to her had hurt most of all.

CHAPTER TEN

THE Durban branch of Aloe Tours had not had a visit from one of its directors in some months, and Amy's unexpected arrival at their offices that Monday morning seemed to send the staff into a disorganised flurry at first, but she was soon bombarded with the problems which could not be dealt with at long distance. It was what she had needed to forget temporarily about Luke, but it proved a long, exhausting day of listening, advising, and making suggestions for future tours to alleviate the difficulties she had encountered on the first one.

Amy's flight to Cape Town left at five o'clock that afternoon. She was tired and she could not wait to get home, but they were delayed for an hour in East London because of technical problems. It was annoying, but there was nothing anyone could do except sit in the airless Boeing and wait until the fault had been repaired by the ground crew. It was nine thirty when the taxi dropped her off at her flat that evening, and Amy was almost dropping with fatigue in the lift that took her up to the fourth floor.

She inserted her key in the lock, turned it, and pushed open the door. She carried her bag inside and she closed the door behind her with her foot before she noticed that something was not as it ought to be. The table lamp had been switched on in the lounge, and a man was rising from his reclining position on the cane bench. Amy's heart and lungs seemed to stop functioning with a violent thud, and a numbness surged into her limbs. A scream rose inside her but paralysis gripped her throat choking off the sound. She was a fraction of a second away from fainting when she realised that the intruder was Luke. Her heart shuddered back to life, and the rush of blood into her head made her ears sing.

'I'm sorry, Amy,' Luke apologised, his narrowed gaze on her ashen face as she sagged limply against the wall behind her. 'I didn't intend to frighten the life out of you.'

Amy's recovery was aided by a fierce surge of anger. 'What the hell are you doing here, and how did you get in?'

'Your caretaker likes his bottle of whisky,' he told her with a hint of a smile curving his sensuous mouth.

'You gave that poor old man a bottle of whisky to let you into my flat?' Sparks of fury flashed in her dark eyes. 'That's bribery!'

'So I bribed him a little,' Luke shrugged carelessly, drawing her attention to the white shirt which fitted tightly across his wide shoulders, and the buttons which were undone almost to his waist to expose far too much of his tanned, hair-matted chest for her own comfort.

'*Why*, Luke?' she demanded, dragging her eyes away from his disturbing male body. 'What do you want?'

'I want you.'

Amy stiffened with a renewed surge of anger. He had forced himself on her the day before, only to reject her when she had surrendered. Fourteen hours ago he had snubbed her in the hotel restaurant, and now he suddenly wanted her. *How dare he!* How dare he stand there and blandly announce that he wanted her after what had happened between them!

'This isn't the time for jokes,' she rebuked him in an icy voice. 'I've just flown in from Durban, I'm tired, and I'm not in the best of moods after a one-hour delay in East London.'

'I'm not joking, Amy,' he bit out the words, his gaze probing her rigid features. 'If you think I wasn't affected by what happened yesterday, then you're wrong. I've been going through hell at the thought of my caddish behaviour, and I simply have to talk to you.'

Her mouth quivered, and she was perilously close to tears when she turned her back on him to fling her handbag on to a chair. 'I don't think we have anything left to talk about.'

'Well, I've got plenty to say, and there's a hell of a lot I want to hear from you!' he contradicted harshly, his hand heavy on her shoulder as he spun her round to face him, but she was too angry at that moment to notice his oddly tortured expression. 'I've been driven nearly out of my mind these past two months trying to find a way to get close to you, and I understand a lot more since you explained what happened four years ago, but I want to get beyond that barrier you've erected between us. I want to know where I stand with you.'

'So it's a cold-blooded declaration you want, is it?' she almost shouted at him, wrenching herself free of his touch. 'Well, I'll tell you where you stand, Luke Tanner. Not here in my flat, that's for certain, so I suggest you go away and *stay* away this time, as you said you would!'

A deathly silence followed her tirade, but his eyes sparked fire, and she was pulled against him with a force that almost winded her. He set his hard mouth on hers in a savage kiss that parted her lips, and she was spinning into a helpless vortex of emotions she could not control. She tried to resist him, but she no longer had the strength to do so, and that hard body against her own sent a weakness surging through her that made her cling to his shoulders for support. She could fight him verbally, but physically and emotionally she was no match for him, and she was trembling violently when at last he released her.

'Tell me now, if you can, that you want me to go away and stay away!' he demanded, his eyes blazing yellow fire into hers.

Her anger had been turned off as if someone had flicked a switch to douse the furnace which had produced it, and she felt as if she had been drained of every scrap of energy she possessed. She stared helplessly up into Luke's eyes, at the hair growing so strongly away from his ruggedly handsome features, and that firmly compressed mouth which had forced hers into submission only a moment ago. She knew that if she sent him away now, she would never see him again, and she had to face the appalling truth that she did not want to live without him.

'*Tell me, Amy!*' His hands gripped her shoulders painfully. 'Tell me to go away, if you can!'

'I—I can't, I——' Her head sagged forward, and her body went limp beneath those strong, supporting hands. 'Oh God, I'm so tired,' she whispered. 'All I want to do is have a hot bath and go to bed.'

Luke tipped her face up and studied her pale, haunted face with narrowed eyes. 'Did you have anything to eat on the plane?'

'They served a meal but I wasn't very hungry.' Even now the thought of food nauseated her.

'Go and have your bath, Amy,' he instructed, giving her a gentle push towards the bathroom, 'and while you're bathing I'll make a couple of sandwiches and coffee.'

She shook her head. She could not allow Luke to go to that much trouble for her, and she was afraid that she would not be able to eat a thing.

'Go on!' he insisted sternly. 'If you don't go now, I'll put you in that bath myself.'

He meant it too, and a tired ghost of a smile touched her mouth as she turned away from him. 'I'm going.'

She took slacks and a sweater into the bathroom with her and closed the door behind her. She did not lock it, she never did, and the thought that Luke might walk in on her never crossed her mind at that moment. She opened the taps to let her bath water run while she took off her creased linen suit and the white blouse which had lost its crispness half-way through the day in Durban's humid climate. Oh, Lord, but she was tired!

Amy sprinkled bathsalts into the water, and soaked for a while before soaping herself. She slid down into the water again and relaxed. Luke was moving about in the kitchen. She could hear the refrigerator door being opened and closed, and she heard a knife clattering on to a plate, but she was so delightfully drowsy that she was too lazy to move. What did Luke want to talk to her about? What was there to say?

'Amy?' Luke's voice roused her some minutes later. 'Are you going to sleep in that bath?'

'Almost,' she admitted, getting out of the bath and taking off the shower cap which had protected her hair.

She had taken down the bathsheet, and she was dabbing her face dry when the door opened. Her heart almost stopped beating as she stood there holding the bathsheet protectively in front of her damp, naked body. She stared at Luke, incapable of speech, and her body quivering with a new tension. What did he want?

'Relax, my dear,' he smiled as if he had read her thoughts. 'You're almost dead on your feet and all I want to do is help you.'

'I—I can m-manage,' she stammered foolishly, too afraid suddenly to move.

'Sure you can,' Luke nodded soberly, removing the bathsheet from fingers that no longer had the strength to cling to it and wrapping it around her body.

She stood petrified while he dried her, his hands firm through the towelling material, and slowly she began to relax. He was treating her like a child, a very tired child, and the last segment of fear and embarrassment deserted her.

He left the bathsheet draped around her to take her robe off the hook behind the door, and he held it up between them. 'Slip into this.'

'My clothes——'

'Forget about your clothes!' he interrupted her authoritatively and, lowering the bathsheet, she quickly slipped her arms into the wide sleeves of her silk robe.

Amy wrapped it about her body, but it was Luke who tied the belt about her waist. He lifted her in his arms—the desire to struggle had long since deserted her—and carried her from the bathroom into the bedroom. She could feel the muscles rippling from his shoulders into his arms, and his face was so close to hers that she merely had to turn her head a fraction to brush her lips against his cheek. Her heart thudded against her ribs, and his arms tightened about her for a brief instant as if he had felt it, then he lowered her gently on to the bed and arranged the pillows comfortably behind her back.

'Stay there and don't move,' he told her, striding out of her room.

Amy could not have moved even if she had wanted to. She felt too pleasantly relaxed, and her mind was too busy assessing the many facets of Luke's character.

His public image had been known to her long before she had met him. His success in business could be attributed to his brilliant mind and ruthless determination, and she knew that he could be equally ruthless and determined in his personal pursuits. He was a harsh man, and yet there was a gentle side to him which she was convinced not many people were aware of. Janet Hawkins would know. Amy had seen the tenderness in the smile Luke has bestowed upon Janet, and he would be gentle with the woman he loved.

She closed her eyes to fight off the pain, and when she opened them again Luke was walking into her bedroom with two mugs of coffee and a plate of sandwiches on a tray. He placed their coffee on the bedside cupboard, and the plate of sandwiches was deposited in Amy's lap before he disposed of the tray.

'I can't possibly eat all this!' she protested, her eyes widening at the amount of cheese and tomato sandwiches on the plate.

'Shut up and eat it!' he said, seating himself beside her, and Amy had a feeling that he would personally shovel every morsel of food into her mouth if she did not do as she was told.

She bit into the first sandwich, not quite sure whether her stomach would accept or reject it, but she soon disovered that she was actually very hungry.

Under Luke's watchful eyes she miraculously succeeded in emptying the plate. She drank her coffee and then he removed the mugs and the plate, seating himself beside her again with that lazy smile in his tawny eyes.

'Feeling better?' he asked quietly.

'Much better,' she sighed, relaxing against the pillows and looking up at him with grave, tired eyes. There was something she had to know, but how was she going to ask him? The silence lengthened between them, disturbed only by the muted sound of the occasional traffic in the street below, and throwing caution to the wind at last she said bluntly, 'Tell me about Janet?'

'Janet Hawkins?' His heavy eyebrows rose a fraction in surprise. 'Janet and Garth and I have known each other ever since I can remember. She's like a sister to me, and she has always treated me like a brother.'

That explained everything, and her heart skipped a joyous beat. 'I guess, then, that there's no truth in the rumour that you never married because all these years you've been in love with Janet?'

'My God!' He looked incredulous. 'Is that what people have been saying?'

'Janet's name was never mentioned,' she corrected, 'but I believe they said you were in love with the girl who had married your best friend, and Janet and Garth fitted that description.'

'I see.' His eyes were hooded, but his mouth twitched as if he was suppressing a smile. 'I think I can imagine what you must have thought when you saw the way Janet and I greeted each other each time we met. Did you believe that rumour was true?'

Amy coloured with embarrassment and guilt. 'Yes, I'm afraid I did.'

'If you'd questioned me about it I wouldn't have withheld the truth from you.'

'I didn't have the right to pry into your personal life, and I still don't, but I——' She swallowed nervously and lowered her eyes. 'I had to know now.'

'Why now?'

His abrupt query drove her into a corner of her own making. How could she explain without betraying her feelings and making a complete idiot of herself?

'My curiosity got the better of me,' she finally evaded the truth, then guilt took over, and she raised her eyes to his to find him studying her intently. 'I'm sorry about the way I behaved yesterday. I was tired and overwrought, and I'm sorry I made you angry.'

'For God's sake, Amy, don't apologise!' he exploded, looking away. 'I can't tell you what a cad I felt afterwards, and I simply couldn't face you this morning.'

'Is that why you left without saying goodbye?' she asked softly, understanding beginning to ease the pain she had suffered.

'Yes.'

'But you bribed the caretaker to let you into my flat, and you waited here for me this evening.'

'I had to talk to you.' He turned his head to look at her, and his strong features looked pale and grim in the dimness of the bedside light. 'I had to make you understand that no way am I going to walk out of your life.'

Her throat tightened, but the corners of her mouth lifted in a tender, yet faintly cynical smile as she held his glance. 'You mean, not for a while anyway.'

'Not for quite a while,' he said, his grim features

relaxing into a smile, and there was something in his eyes that found an echo in her soul but it was Luke who broke the spell. 'Get into bed, my dear, and go to sleep. I'll put out the lights and lock the door behind me.'

Amy had never loved him more than at that moment. She had also never wanted him more. His concern for her was the most touching thing she had ever encountered, and everything else faded in the wake of that astounding knowledge that she did not want him to leave. She wanted him to stay, she wanted him to make love to her, and pride and self-respect were suddenly no more than words she had read somewhere.

'Luke!' Her hand clutched at his arm when he would have risen, and she raised appealing eyes to his. 'Please don't go.'

His arm tensed beneath her fingers, and his glance sharpened. She sensed the uncertainty in him, and it was there in the tawny eyes probing hers. 'You're tired, and you don't know what you're saying.'

He was, strangely, giving her the opportunity to change her mind, but she shook her head as she sat up and placed a tentative, caressing hand against his rough cheek. 'You don't really believe that, do you?'

'I want to believe it,' he said, rigid beneath her touch. 'I don't think I can stand the torment of wanting you and not having you.'

'Poor Luke,' she whispered tenderly. 'I have made you suffer, haven't I?'

The desire to touch him was so intense that she undid the remainder of his shirt buttons and slid her hands inside. His warm, hairy skin made her palms tingle, and she explored his chest with a daring she had never known before.

'Amy!' His voice was like a deep roll of thunder and unmistakable fires were beginning to dance in his eyes. 'You do know what you're doing to me, don't you?'

Yes, she knew. She could feel his heart thudding even though his body was tense with the effort to control himself, and her own body was beginning to ache for his touch.

'Make love to me, Luke,' she pleaded shamelessly in a choked whisper. 'I want you, and I can't fight it any more.'

A nerve was jumping along the side of his jaw when she pulled his shirt out of his slacks, and she felt him tremble beneath her hands as she continued to explore his powerful chest. His eyes darkened, and suddenly she was in his arms with his plundering mouth drawing an instant and unashamed response from hers. His hands were moving convulsively against her back, his touch like fire through the flimsy barrier of her silk robe, and then he was lowering her back on to the pillows.

'Amy, Amy, Amy!' Her name sounded almost like a benediction when he buried his face against her throat where his warm lips could feel the erratic beat of her pulse. 'I can't!' he groaned.

Amy felt an icy coldness surging through her body. 'Don't you . . . want me any more?'

'I want you, my love,' he set her mind at rest in a voice that was not quite steady. 'I want to touch you and kiss you all over. I want every inch of your lovely body to come alive for me, and I don't want to stop until it does.'

'Then, why?' she asked, looking bewildered when he raised his head.

'Do you remember what I said to you that night on the *Amazon*?' He had said so many things which she had not taken seriously, and he smiled down into her bewildered eyes as he released her and sat up to comb his fingers through his hair. 'I said I'd have to marry you first,' he reminded her, 'and I meant it, Amy. I want to marry you, if you'll have me.'

Amy's heart came to a lurching halt before it raced on again at a suffocating speed. Oh, how cruel of him if he was merely joking!

'You—you want to m-marry me?'

'Yes, Amy,' he answered her gravely. 'I want to marry you, and all I'm asking for is the opportunity to make you love me a little.'

Amy could not decide whether to laugh or cry. He was so heart-wrenchingly unsure of her and her ability to love again that he was asking for no more than the opportunity to make her love him a little.

Tenderness rose inside her like a warm, glowing tide. 'Do you love me, Luke?'

'I've loved you from the moment I first saw you,' he confessed, taking her hand in his and bringing it to his lips. 'I went home that night and telephoned my mother like an excited child to tell her that I'd at last met the woman I wanted to spend the rest of my life with.'

It all sounded too marvellously wonderful to be true, and her eyes widened incredulously. 'Your mother has known all this time how you feel about me?'

'Does it matter?' he asked anxiously.

'I feel a little jealous that she knew it before I did,' she teased him with a new-found freedom.

'You dear, sweet idiot!' he laughed, then his expression sobered. 'Will you marry me?'

'Yes, Luke,' she said without hesitation.

'Thank God!' he sighed, making her realise exactly how anxious he had been that she might refuse him. 'When?' he rapped out the next query.

'Whenever you say,' she answered accommodatingly.

'This coming Saturday?'

Her eyes widened. He was moving too fast, but when she looked up into his agitated eyes she knew that it was what she wanted as well.

'I think I'd like that,' she nodded, and he sighed deeply.

'That's settled, then.'

'Not quite,' she smiled, curling her fingers against his cheek when he pressed his lips into her palm, and there was a query in the eyes that met hers. 'Do we have to wait until Saturday?'

'I don't think I could,' he smiled down into her flushed face. 'I merely wanted you to know that what I had in mind for you was something permanent.'

Her heart felt as if it wanted to burst with happiness, and she flung her arms about his neck with a joyous exclamation on her lips. 'Oh, Luke, darling, I love you!'

Amy felt him stiffen against her, then he loosened her arms about his neck and held her away from him. 'You don't mean it! You *can't* mean it!' he said, his eyes burning down into hers with a probing intensity.

'I'm afraid I do,' she confessed, letting him see into her heart for the first time. 'I love you, and I think I must have loved you from the start, but I knew for sure that night after I had dinner at your home with you and your mother.'

'Amy, sweetheart!' She was gathered against him, and he was raining passionate little kisses on her upturned face before his hungry mouth claimed hers in a heart-stopping kiss. 'I love you, I want you, and God knows I need you.'

His hands were impatient as he parted her robe

and slid it off her shoulders, and his warm mouth trailed fiery kisses along her throat and shoulder, stirring to life an answering flame inside her.

'Did I do this?' he asked throatily, fingering the dark discoloration on her shoulders.

'I bruise easily,' she tried to make light of it, but there was something so erotic about his tongue caressing those tender bruises that her breath caught in her throat.

The clean male smell of him intoxicated her almost as much as the touch of his hands on her body, and her own hands were equally eager to explore the hollows and planes of his muscled back. He discarded his clothes, and his naked body against her own inflamed her.

Luke aroused her slowly, his mouth and his hands trailing over her receptive body as he fulfilled his promise to make every part of her come alive for him, and in the process Luke was teaching her things about herself which she had never known. He caressed her deeply and intimately, raising her excitement and pleasure to a peak where it was so intense she was convinced that she would die if he did not take her now, but still he held back.

'Touch me, Amy,' he instructed hoarsely, his hand guiding hers down his body, and a low, shuddering groan escaped him when she followed the action through.

She touched him as she had never dared to touch a man before, and her own excitement was intensified as she explored his body in much the same way he had explored hers. His breathing was laboured beneath her ministrations, and a low, animal-like growl escaped him when he finally took possession of her.

There was nothing gentle about his lovemaking,

it was a savage, thrusting intrusion, but her body welcome it, revelled in it, and her pleasure intensified, rising higher and higher like mercury in a thermometer.

A husky cry of pleasure escaped her as that achingly sweet tension snapped inside her, and she was instantly flung into a storm-tossed ocean where wave after wave of the most exquisite sensations washed over her.

Luke groaned and sagged heavily against her and for long, endless seconds the only sound she could hear was their thundering heartbeats and laboured breathing.

Amy was speechless with wonder. She could not believe what had happened to her, and she could only cling to Luke in the sweet aftermath of their lovemaking.

'I never knew it could be quite like this,' she finally confessed in an awed whisper when she lay in the circle of his strong arms with her head nestling against his shoulder.

'Didn't you?' he asked, and she felt him smile before he turned his head to kiss her tenderly on the forehead.

'But, then, you're an experienced lover,' she pointed out.

'And that pleased you very much, didn't it?' he mocked her, but for the first time she did not object to his mockery.

'Yes and no.'

'What kind of answer is that?' he demanded laughingly.

'I don't like thinking about all those other women,' she answered him with a dash of truth wrapped up in her teasing words.

'Jealous?'

'Yes,' she admitted without hesitation.

'You don't have to be. None of those women meant anything to me,' he assured her, tipping up her face and kissing her firmly on the lips. 'Should I be jealous of the fact that you loved someone else before me?'

'No,' she murmured soberly. Luke did not say anything more, he simply kissed her hard on the lips once again and stretched out an arm to switch off the bedside light.

Amy went to sleep almost immediately, but she awoke with a start during the night, convinced that she had dreamt everything. She went cold, her hand reaching out, and her relief was almost an agony when she felt Luke's warm body on the bed beside her.

She slipped out of bed, taking care not to wake him, and put on her robe. She walked across the room, and carefully drew the curtains aside at the window. It was two o'clock in the morning, and the street was empty and strangely deserted at that hour. *Empty and deserted*, her thoughts echoed through her mind, and her fears returned partially when she realised that *that* was how she had felt all these years. Four years ago she had had no one but Uncle Ben, and he had been a virtual stranger to her when he had come up to Johannesburg to fetch her. She had written to him after her mother had died, telling him of the death of his only sister, and afterwards the occasional letter had passed between them. She had written to him again several weeks after Keith had died, telling him about the baby she had lost and pouring her agony out on paper to someone who had been almost a stranger had been easier than talking about it. Now there was Luke, and if she should lose him . . .! She shuddered at the thought, wrapping her arms about herself as if to shut out that terrible fear.

'Amy?'

She turned round at the sound of Luke's voice, and blinked to adjust her eyes to the bedside light he had switched on. With his hair tousled and his eyes still filled with sleep he looked almost boyish, and her love for him was almost a physical pain wrenching at her heart.

'Why aren't you asleep?'

'I should be asking you that question,' he grinned at her as he pushed himself up on one elbow, and he looked magnificent lying there with nothing but a sheet covering the lower half of his body.

'I woke up and—and I was suddenly afraid.' There was a flash of understanding in his eyes and, flinging the sheet aside, he got up and came to her. He opened his arms, and she went into them, finding comfort in burying her face against his broad chest, and inhaling the manly fragrance of him. 'Don't leave me, Luke. Please don't ever leave me,' she whispered anxiously, locking her arms about his waist in an almost convulsive action.

'Don't be afraid, my darling,' he murmured into her hair. 'I can't promise you not to die, but I can promise that I shall never leave you while I'm alive.'

'I love you, Luke,' she sighed, raising tear-filled eyes to his. 'I love you more than I can ever tell you.'

Her own feelings were mirrored in his eyes as he lowered his head and kissed her with a tenderness that stirred her deeply.

'Come back to bed, my love,' he said, his arm still firmly about her as he drew her away from the window. She took off her robe and got into bed and snuggled up close to Luke when he switched off the light. 'Do you think Ben could spare you for a couple of weeks?' he asked unexpectedly, turning towards her and drawing her body into the curve of his.

'I'm sure something could be arranged,' she said, feeling a little bewildered. 'Why do you ask?'

'I was thinking of a honeymoon in Switzerland,' Luke murmured, his lips nuzzling her throat and sending a shiver of pleasure through her. 'With all that snow about we could ski if we wanted to, or we could spend most of our time in the chalet making love. Would you like that?'

'It sounds wonderful,' she agreed, her body responding to the touch of his hand trailing down across her hip and thigh and up again to cup her breast. Oh, how easily he aroused that aching need, and it was still too incredible to believe that he wanted to give up his cherished freedom to marry her. 'Do you really love me, Luke? she whispered anxiously.

'Would you like me to show you how much?' he asked, an unmistakable hint of sensuality in his voice that quickened her pulse.

'Yes, please,' she breathed, locking her arms about him when he leaned over her.

His mouth found hers in the darkness, and then the magic started all over again. If there were fears lingering in her mind, then they faded swiftly in the storm of love and passion that swept through her. In less than a week she would be Luke's wife, and with him at her side she would no longer be afraid of loving.

ROMANCE

ROMANCE

Next month's romances from Mills & Boon

Each month, you can choose from a world of variety in romance with Mills & Boon. These are the new titles to look out for next month.

THE TULLAGINDI RODEO Kerry Allyne
WALK INTO TOMORROW Rosemary Carter
DANCING IN THE DARK Pippa Clarke
HIDDEN TREASURES Emma Goldrick
PLAIN JANE Rosemary Hammond
TRY TO REMEMBER Vanessa James
MAID TO MEASURE Roberta Leigh
PASSIONATE VENGEANCE Margaret Mayo
BACHELOR IN PARADISE Elizabeth Oldfield
BITTER LEGACY Sandra K. Rhoades
*THE GLASS MADONNA Liza Manning
*FANCY FREE Karen van der Zee

Buy them from your usual paperback stockist, or write to: Mills & Boon Reader Service, P.O. Box 236, Thornton Rd, Croydon, Surrey CR9 3RU, England. Readers in South Africa — write to: Independent Book Services Pty, Postbag X3010, Randburg, 2125, S. Africa.

*These two titles are available *only* from Mills & Boon Reader Service.

Mills & Boon
the rose of romance

Family honour in Spain, ex-husband in Greece, society life in England and the sands of Arabia.

To celebrate the introduction of four new Mills & Boon authors, we are delighted to offer a unique presentation of four love stories that are guaranteed to capture your heart.

LOVE'S GOOD FORTUNE by Louise Harris
THE FINAL PRICE by Patricia Wilson
SWEET POISON by Angela Wells
PERFUMES OF ARABIA by Sara Wood

Priced £4.80, this attractively packaged set of new titles will be available from August 1986.